MAGIC & MONSTERS

STARRY HOLLOW WITCHES, BOOK 12

ANNABEL CHASE

CHAPTER ONE

"GOOD MORNING, MY MOON AND STARS," I said, sweeping into the office of *Vox Populi* with a cinnamon latte and a sunny smile.

Bentley Smith glanced up from his computer screen, deep lines of suspicion creasing his brow. "Does this mean you finally got a full night's sleep? If not, I'd like to request a desk change."

"Oh, please. One cranky day and you act like I'm a menace to society." I'd been plagued by nightmares this week and unable to sleep through the night. I finally understood what Marley must've gone through. It seemed like only yesterday that my daughter was curled up in bed beside me, smacking me in the face with a wayward hand and encroaching on my personal space.

Bentley pointed to his chin. "This mark is going to scar."

"I threw a stress ball, Bentley, not a stapler." I eased into my chair at the neighboring desk. "If you must know, I tried a sleeping potion that Linnea recommended and it worked like a charm." Generally, I was hesitant to take any kind of sleep aid when I was the only adult in the house. I didn't

1

want to put Marley in a vulnerable position where she discovered me unconscious and was unable to be roused. An incident like that could result in hours of therapy in the future. That being said, a mother on the verge of a mental breakdown due to lack of sleep could result in years of therapy, not hours, so I chose the cheaper option and drank the potion.

"I'm glad you took the potion. Self-care is important," Tanya said. The office manager fluttered from the supply closet to her desk.

"I think we can agree that we all benefit from a rested Ember," Bentley said. "Especially me."

I booted up my computer. "Stop exaggerating."

"Exaggerating? Yesterday you threatened to reshape my ears with the help of a hole puncher." He rubbed the point of his elfin ear. "I'd prefer not to live in fear."

I popped the lid off my cup and blew off the steam before taking a careful sip of my latte. Yesterday I scalded my tongue on the way here, which *may* have contributed to my attitude toward Bentley. I wasn't ready to swear a blood oath to it, but I was open to the possibility.

"Where's the boss?" I asked. Alec Hale was the editor-in-chief of the paper as well as my handsome vampire boyfriend. It was easy to look forward to coming to work when I knew I'd get to lay eyes on his exquisite vampiric form. I craned my neck to see whether his office door was open or closed. Hmm. Closed.

"He's been holed up in there since before I arrived," Tanya said, following my gaze. "I think he's working on a new book."

I frowned. "A new book?" He was purportedly three-quarters of the way through his current work-in-progress, which was why we hadn't been spending that much time together lately. He couldn't possibly have finished that quickly. Epic fantasy took epic hours to write.

Tanya leaned over and lowered her voice. "I don't mean to alarm you, but I heard him laughing."

My hand froze with the edge of the cup only millimeters from my lip. "Laughing? Alec?" The stoic vampire wasn't known for belting out the laughs and certainly not over his fantasy world where everything was dire and fates were forever hanging in the balance. "How would you categorize it?"

Tanya licked her lips, thinking. "More of a guffaw."

I shot a quizzical look at Bentley. "Did you hear this alleged guffaw?"

His head dipped. "I did."

I pushed back my chair. "And no one thought to check on him?"

"He's your boyfriend," Bentley said accusingly.

I started toward the back office. "And he's your editor-in-chief. If he's guffawing, you should want to know why." I harrumphed. "Some inquisitive reporter you are."

"No one's writing a story on what makes Alec Hale laugh," Bentley grumbled.

"Well, maybe they should be!" I straightened my shirt before rapping on the door. "Little pig, little pig, won't you let me come in?" I didn't wait for a response. I clicked open the door and poked my head inside.

Alec stared at his laptop screen with a lopsided grin. His brilliant green eyes met mine and the grin broadened. "Perfect. Just the face I wanted to see."

"According to reliable sources, you've been holed up in here for hours and laughing to yourself like a deranged hyena. What are you working on?"

He dragged a hand through his golden blond hair. "I had

an idea for a new book the other day and the muse refused to let me go."

I moved to peer over his shoulder at the screen. "What's it about?"

"A supernatural agent that hunts demons," he said.

"That sounds fun."

"Yes, and she's a self-loathing fury."

"Ooh, dangerous." I perched on the edge of his desk. "And funny, too, from the sound of it."

"She is. And she has this insane family." He chuckled to himself. "I'm basing the grandmother on a more ill-mannered version of Hyacinth, but please don't tell her. The comparison won't be flattering."

I pretended to button my lip. "I'm glad you're having fun with it."

He reached for my knee and tugged me closer. "You'll never guess who inspired the fury."

"I'm not sure I know what a fury is." I'd have to ask Marley. She was my own personal Google, although she'd told me repeatedly that Google itself was actually my own personal Google.

His hand traveled up my thigh. "She's smart and sexy and sassy and very powerful."

"My kind of woman."

"And mine." He gazed at me with a sexy smile that made my stomach flutter.

I bent forward and brushed my lips against his. "I've missed you at the cottage. Marley too."

"And I've missed you." His lips lingered on mine and I enjoyed the taste of fresh strawberries. He withdrew and sighed contentedly. "I'm glad you're here. Did Linnea's potion work?"

"If I had any nightmares, they didn't wake me." Linnea had wanted to know more about the nightmares so that she could mix the right potion, but I couldn't tell her that they started after I opened our ancestor Ivy Rose's Book of Shadows. If I told Linnea, that increased the risk that Aunt Hyacinth would find out and the older witch was the last paranormal I wanted to know. Thankfully, the concoction seemed to do the trick without the need for details.

"Good, then I can brief you on your new assignment."

"I have one?" The lazy part of me had hoped to skate by this week as I attempted to recover from my bouts of disrupted sleep.

"You do. A very good one, in fact. Expect a disgruntled response from Bentley."

Uh oh. "Are you sure you don't want to let him have the story?"

He brought my hand to his mouth and left a trail of butterfly kisses across my knuckle. "Trust me. You want this one. It's a once-in-a-lifetime opportunity. Marley will be interested too."

His fang gently pricked the skin on my hand and a small gasp escaped me. How did he manage to make that feel so erotic? I pushed the heel of my hand against his forehead.

"Down, boy, before I straddle you right here."

He cocked an eyebrow. "You're not exactly persuading me to stop with talk like that."

I took a few steps backward to put physical distance between the vampire's seductive charm and me.

"Why don't you tell me about the assignment in the safety of the main office?" I asked. Where I was guaranteed to remain fully clothed and appropriate.

Alec rose to his feet and adjusted his cufflinks. "That's a splendid idea."

I hurried back to my desk and scooped up my latte for a greedy sip. Ah, it was now the ideal temperature. Flirting with my boss had multiple advantages.

Alec stood in front of our desks. "I have exciting news to share with everyone. I'm sure you're familiar with Winston York."

"He's a legend," Tanya said.

"Of course," Bentley added. "Who isn't? You'd have to be living under a rock not to know."

Slowly, I raised my hand. "Who's Winston York?"

Bentley rolled his eyes. "Or from New Jersey."

"Winston York is the most famous creature hunter in the world and he lives right here in Starry Hollow," Tanya said.

I cringed. "He hunts magical creatures? That's terrible."

"No, hunts them as in he tracks them down," Alec said. "He doesn't hurt them. He's only interested in recording them to share with the world."

"He doesn't do it anymore though," Bentley said. "He retired last year."

Alec clasped his hands in front of him. "That's part of the big news. It seems he's come out of seclusion."

"Why now?" I asked.

"There's been a sighting of a tepen right here in Starry Hollow," Alec said.

Tanya and Bentley lit up like someone just told them they'd won front row tickets to a Bruce Springsteen concert. Well, it's how they'd light up if they loved the Boss as much as I did.

"What's a tepen?" I asked.

Bentley groaned and buried his face in his hands.

"You'll have ample time to learn as you'll be covering the story," Alec said.

The elf's face drained of color, leaving his freckles even more pronounced. "You're assigning the story to Ember?"

"Hyacinth insisted on it," Alec said with a shrug that said 'what can you do?' At least that explained Alec's willingness to give me the story. Bentley was much more suited to covering a story about the David Attenborough of the paranormal world. I tended to fall asleep watching nature shows that featured the actual David Attenborough, much to Marley's dismay.

Bentley folded his arms in a huff. "What am I supposed to work on this week while the rookie is covering the best story we've had in years?"

"I have no doubt you'll find a worthy topic," Alec said.

Bentley's sigh was louder than he intended and he immediately swiveled his chair around to avoid making eye contact with Alec.

"Where can I find this wonder of the world?" I asked.

"The tepen is elusive," Alec said.

"I meant the old dude."

"Ah, Winston will be at Balefire Beach later today to record a segment," Alec said. "He's agreed to meet with you there."

I gulped down the rest of my latte. "Should I bring any protective gear? How dangerous is this creature?"

"I doubt you'll be seeing the tepen," Alec said. "As I said, it's elusive. It won't be parading along the beach."

"The tepen is an incredibly rare type of sea serpent," Bentley said with a trace of bitterness. "You might want to research it before you show up and embarrass yourself."

"Nah, I prefer to wing it. Makes life more interesting." I chucked my empty cup in the garbage can.

Bentley simmered in anger and resentment. "She won't do the story justice, Alec."

"Then I suggest you take it up with Hyacinth," Alec said.

Bentley recoiled. Nobody in their right mind wanted to take up anything with Hyacinth Rose-Muldoon. She was the intimidating owner of the weekly newspaper, the wealthy grand dame of Starry Hollow society, a descendant of the One True Witch, and, most importantly, my aunt.

"I'll find my own story," Bentley mumbled, his head bent in resignation.

As tempting as it was, I resisted the urge to gloat. Bentley looked far too miserable. "Cheer up," I said. "I bet your story will end up being way cooler than mine." I burst into laughter. "Who am I kidding? My story is the Marcia to your Jan." Okay, so resistance was futile.

Bentley glowered at me. "Mine will be the talk of the town. You'll see."

"Yeah, sure. Have fun writing up the Lost Items column. Oh, and don't forget to include your dignity."

CHAPTER TWO

I STOOD outside the front door of Rose Cottage with my aging Yorkshire terrier on a leash. Prescott Peabody III, or PP3 as he was affectionately known, sniffed the grass like he was checking for bombs in the field during World War II.

"Hey, buddy. If you could hurry things along because I'm kind of on a tight schedule today," I said. I wasn't sure why I bothered to say anything. The Yorkie moved at his own agitatingly slow pace, like an old lady with a walker crossing a busy intersection.

A familiar witch on a bicycle came into view and I urged PP3 to finish his business. I didn't want to be late for my lesson with Marigold, the coven's Mistress of Psychic Skills. She'd insist on sticking to the full hour and then I'd be late for my meeting with Winston York.

The witch was pedaling so furiously that I expected her to rise into the air like Miss Gulch in *The Wizard of Oz*. She screeched to a halt at the gate and leaned the bicycle against the fence.

I inclined my head toward the Yorkie. "I have the perfect little dog for your wicker basket."

Marigold frowned. "Is this one of your pop culture references?" She marched up the walkway like the drill sergeant she secretly wanted to be.

"It's not one of *my* references. *The Wizard of Oz* belongs to everyone." PP3 finally peed and I leaned down to give him a reaffirming pat on the head. "Who's a good boy? That's right. You are."

Marigold adjusted the hem of her pink cotton sweater. "Are you ready or do you need a few more minutes to spoil that canine creature?"

"We need to finish on time today because I have to meet some guy at the beach."

Marigold arched an eyebrow. "Does Alec know about this?"

"I didn't meet him on Tinder. It's a work assignment. I need to interview Winston York."

Marigold threw up a hand to steady herself against the front door. "Wait, you have an interview with *the* Winston York?"

"That's right." I crouched down to unleash the dog.

She gaped at me in disbelief. "But he's a hermit now. He doesn't give interviews anymore."

I pushed open the door and nudged the dog inside. "Apparently he's breaking his silence for the sake of nature nerds everywhere."

The witch grabbed my arm. "Take me with you."

"I'm talking to an old man about a messed-up sea serpent. How interesting can it be?"

"You have no idea," Marigold said.

"Clearly."

"For a man his age, he still manages to be devastatingly rugged and handsome."

"Years in the wild will do that to a guy, I guess."

Marigold fanned herself and I felt a surge of pride when I noticed that she was wearing the bracelet I made for her that protects against menopausal symptoms. "I used to have the most elaborate fantasies about what would happen if he tracked me deep in the woods and wrestled me to the ground."

I held my hands over my ears. "And I think we're done here."

She jostled my elbow. "Come on then. You can't risk being late. Let's get our lesson out of the way."

Together we traipsed to the woods behind the cottage where she preferred to hold the lessons. Although she claimed it was because of her great love for the outdoors, I suspected it was because she worried I'd destroy the interior of Rose Cottage with my misguided attempts to perform psychic magic.

"How's the bracelet working out for you?" I asked.

The witch smiled. "Really well, actually. Whatever you did, I'm impressed. You'd better be careful, I mentioned it to a few friends in a similar condition, so you may have a few orders coming in."

I positioned myself in front of one of the live oak trees. "I don't see myself as a jewelry maker. That was a twofer. I got you to stop complaining about your hot flashes and I got Hazel to stop complaining that I don't take her lessons seriously." I rolled up my sleeves. "What's on the agenda today, Mr. Miyagi? If we're waxing on and waxing off, we should probably start with your chin and upper lip."

Marigold narrowed her eyes. "Hormonal changes will do that. Just you wait, Ember. A few more years and you won't think it's so amusing."

"I don't think it's amusing now. I already have a clown named Hazel that makes me feel like I'm being taught circus tricks. No need to add the bearded lady."

She folded her arms. "Let's get started before I decide to do a body swap and embarrass you beyond repair."

I balked. "I'm sorry. Do a what now?"

"Body swap."

"You can Freaky Friday me? Why have you never mentioned this before?"

Her smile was full of mischievous confidence. "It's always good practice to keep an ace up your sleeve, Ember. You never know when you might need it."

"You have lipstick on your teeth. You might want to fix that before you meet your celebrity crush."

She rubbed away the pink spots with her finger. "Your aunt requested that we practice astral projection again."

"In case I need to pretend to be a ghost for Halloween? What's the point?"

Marigold shrugged. "It's one of the rarer abilities. She likes the idea of her niece possessing unusual talents so she can boast at the coven meetings."

I waved a hand. "I don't want to astral project. Been there. Got the transparent T-shirt." I paused, thinking about what I said. "Okay, that doesn't quite work, but you get the idea."

She heaved an impatient sigh. "Fine. Which ability would you like to explore today, Ember?"

I motioned between us. "I want you to Freaky Friday me. For the uninformed, that's a movie where a mom and daughter switch bodies. It's hilarious."

"Why would you want that? I would think the idea of occupying an older witch's body would terrify you."

"Well, you wouldn't be my first choice, but I love that movie so much. I want to see if we can actually do it so I can tell Marley." She was a big fan of the movie too.

"We don't have much time and it's challenging." Marigold played with the bracelet on her wrist as she mulled over the request. "On the other hand, I suppose your aunt would be pleased that you're aiming higher than the sofa."

My head bobbed up and down. "Yes. She'd appreciate that I'm making an effort."

"Fine, but if you can't manage it then we need to tick astral projection off today's list. We need to hold hands for this one." Marigold crossed the clearing to clasp my hands in hers.

"Do we? Or is this just as an excuse to get close to me?"

"If this goes well, we'll be closer than you ever thought possible." Her wicked grin made me swallow hard. This suddenly seemed like a bad idea. Maybe I should've stuck with Casper magic. What if we got stuck and couldn't swap back?

"Do I repeat an incantation or what?"

Marigold shushed me. "I'll tell you in a second, Miss Impatient. I'm getting centered." She closed her eyes and I noticed the lines across her forehead deepen.

"What's the matter?"

Her eyes remained closed. "Nothing."

"Liar. Your forehead looks like a toddler's Etch A Sketch."

She squeezed my hands in an effort to silence me. "I'm trying to concentrate. Close your eyes."

I obeyed and tried to focus on my breathing. It wasn't easy. I got distracted by every little sound in the woods. My metaphorical squirrels were now actual ones. Scampering. Singing. Rustling. Whatever the woodland creatures were doing, I was tuned in.

"Feel the magic flow between us," Marigold said in a quiet, soothing voice. It was a far cry from her usual bossy tone.

"No Latin?" I queried.

"Shh. No more talking unless I tell you to repeat after me."

Aaaand there was the bossy witch I knew and tolerated.

"*Mutatio, duo, corporis*," she chanted and squeezed my hands to indicate I should join in.

Energy tickled my palms before spreading to the rest of my extremities. I felt a *snap!* and our hands released. I took a wobbly step back and realized that I was looking at—

Myself.

"Holy Lindsay Lohan," I breathed. "It worked."

She—I—looked down to confirm. "I'm actually shocked we succeeded. I thought for sure it would be a dud."

"Is my voice really that nasal? I sound much sexier in my own head."

Marigold didn't reply. She stared at my hands with a strange intensity.

"They're just hands, Marigold. You have two of them." I waved mine at her and I immediately felt a stab of pain in the thumb joint. "Sheesh. Arthritis too? You're falling apart at the seams."

"We need to switch back. Now." Her tone startled me. She grabbed my hands and repeated the spell to return us to our respective bodies.

I felt another *snap!* and knew without looking that I was home again. My body really was my temple.

"That was short-lived fun," I said. "What happened? You missed your tight hip flexors too much? You should really consider yoga." Not that I was one to talk. I walked around like a wooden plank with feet.

Marigold seemed at a loss for words. "Ember." She hesitated. "Never mind. We should go. You don't want to be late for Winston York. He's as old as the hills. You might never get another chance."

I wanted to inquire about her odd reaction to the spell, but I could tell she wasn't in the frame of mind to discuss the issue.

"Okay, let me run back into the cottage first. I need a snack."

She scrutinized me. "If you needed a snack, you should've gotten one before our lesson."

I hurried back toward the cottage with Marigold beside me. "I always eat after our lesson. I can't change my appetite for one interview."

"No, but you won't starve if you skip it either."

I glared at her. "Hey, you're the one who insisted we do the lesson. We could've skipped that and I could've enjoyed a nice, long snack." I flung open the door to the cottage.

"And risk your aunt's wrath? I don't think so. You know she expects a report."

"Still?" I breezed into the kitchen with Marigold hot on my heels. "You'd think by now she'd let it go."

"When have you known your aunt to let anything go? She's like PP3 with a laundered sock."

Fair enough. I raided the refrigerator for something I could inhale quickly and settled on leftover shrimp and cocktail sauce. There were benefits to living in a coastal town and the food was definitely one of them.

"Why not make something up?" I asked. I swiped the shrimp across the top of the sauce and popped it into my mouth.

"What if I suggested that to you? Don't worry about inter-viewing Winston York, just make something up!"

"He's a recluse. Who would know?" I gobbled down a couple more shrimp.

"It's a moot point now. You've completed the lesson." Marigold's hand hovered over the shrimp. "May I?"

I flicked my hand in the bowl's direction. "Go for it."

A knock on the door took me by surprise. "Come in!" I shoved one last shrimp into my mouth.

My cousin Florian appeared in the kitchen holding a

cardboard box. "Oh, good. You're here. I need your input." He set the box on the counter and pulled out a purple T-shirt. "I have a few options and I'd like your input."

I studied the T-shirt with its image of an adorable smiling serpent with a hawk head wearing sunglasses. The text read *Trippin' with Tepen.*

"How in the world did you get those printed so fast?" I asked.

He tossed the purple top to me and pulled a green T-shirt from the box. It bore a similar image except, instead of sunglasses, the creature was coiled around a cocktail glass and the text read *It's Tepen Time Somewhere.*

"Wow," I said. "You've been busy."

"I figure we can set up a kiosk at the beach and sell them. More money for the tourism board."

"They are superb," Marigold said. "I'd take one of each."

"Thanks." Florian beamed at the older witch. "Mother said they were banal and pedestrian, but she's not our target customer, is she?"

"She's no one's target customer," I muttered. "Listen, you know I love a good T-shirt comparison as much as the next person, but I need to get to the beach and interview Winston York."

He brightened. "Can I come?"

I rolled my eyes. "I'm running late as it is."

"I'll drive," he said. "My car is much faster than yours."

"Deal."

We left the cottage and I slid into Florian's sleek and shiny convertible. "When did you get this one?" I asked.

"Do you like it?" he asked. "I got tired of the other one, so Mother agreed to foot the bill for a new one."

So much for trying to despoil him. "What happens when Mother gets tired of footing the bill for you? Will she trade you in for another son?"

In the seat behind me, Marigold strangled a laugh.

The wheels kicked up dirt as Florian sped down the dirt path away from the cottage. We passed Thornhold and I spotted Aunt Hyacinth berating a gardener on the veranda.

"Maybe we should put the top up," I said.

Florian responded by turning up the radio. Unfortunately, he took the turn onto the main road a little too fast, a move that caught the attention of local authorities. The red flight flashed behind us and I sank against the seat.

"Now I'm really late," I mumbled.

Deputy Bolan sauntered up to the driver's side door with a smirk. The leprechaun seemed especially pleased when he saw the car's occupants.

"Whatever you're going to do, can you do it quickly?" I asked. "I have somewhere to be."

"A chauffeur and an entourage," the deputy said, his gaze flicking to Marigold in the backseat.

"Florian is giving me a ride because his car is faster than mine."

"Clearly."

"I'm trying to get to an assignment for the newspaper," I said. "It's urgent." I rustled through the box at my feet and yanked up a T-shirt triumphantly. "See? There's a tepen and Winston York has emerged from retirement to cover the event."

His beady leprechaun eyes widened to the size of a popcorn kernel. "Are you serious? Why haven't I heard about this?"

"Because no one tells you anything," I said. "That's what happens when you're so judgy."

He glowered at me.

"Is he getting a ticket or what?" I pressed.

Florian turned to me. "Hey! No need to pester him."

"Don't worry, Rose-Muldoon. I won't punish you. You can't help who you're related to."

"Amen to that," I said.

Deputy Bolan tapped the top edge of the door. "Just drive more carefully."

"Thanks, I appreciate it."

As soon as the leprechaun walked away, I smacked Florian's arm. "Pedal to the metal, cousin."

The pealing of wheels was probably the wrong way to demonstrate driving more carefully, but I didn't care. I was already late and I didn't want word to get back to Alec or worse—Aunt Hyacinth. It wouldn't matter that Florian was behind the wheel. It would be all my fault.

We arrived at Balefire Beach and I opened the door before Florian finished parking the car.

"Now you want to rush?" Marigold shook her head and opened the car door.

"I'm running ahead." I bolted for the beach, kicking off my shoes when I reached the sand.

In the distance I saw a portly man in a white shirt and matching trousers on the beach. Not the ruggedly handsome older man I expected based on Marigold's description. I should've known better. His thinning hair was stark white and it was only when we got closer that I realized he was barefoot. So he was eccentric on top of everything else. Excellent.

"Mr. York, hi. I'm Ember Rose." I stuck out my hand. "Sorry I'm late."

He gave my hand a reluctant shake. "Nature waits for no one, Miss Rose, no matter what her pedigree is."

My pedigree? I was competing for Best in Show now? "I wasn't late because I have entitlement issues."

The older man fixed me with a withering stare that would

have given Aunt Hyacinth a run for her money. "Oh, no? Then what other reason is there?"

I struggled for a good answer. "I have organizational issues. I'm chronically late."

"I see. A sign of disrespect and contempt."

Florian and Marigold arrived behind us and I suddenly wished the beach would turn into quicksand. I bet there was a spell for that.

"Um, Mr. York, this is my cousin, Florian, and our coven's Mistress of Psychic Skills, Marigold."

The creature hunter didn't crack a smile. "I have a busy schedule today so that I can adequately prepare. I don't like an audience."

"Oh, I know." Marigold placed a friendly hand on his arm. "I'm a huge fan, Mr. York. I've followed every update you've ever done with keen eyes." She stroked his arm. "And I am so pleased that you've decided to come out of retirement."

"It's only temporary," he said, easing out of reach. "I'm here to capture footage of a rare and wonderful creature and then I'm returning to my hovel to toil away the rest of my days in my workshop while my wife complains about the mess I've left."

Florian snorted. "Sounds about right."

Winston gave him an appraising look. "Are you married young man?"

Marigold and I burst into laughter and Florian's cheeks colored. "No, sir," he said. "Haven't met my match yet."

"I'm waiting for him to discover his reflection," I said.

The wizard shot me a deadly look. "And where is the tepen?" he asked.

"Not here, unfortunately," Winston said. "I've made notes and I'm planning to record in this area before moving on to the next spot."

"I'd love to help if you need a hand," Marigold said. "I'm very handsy...I mean, handy."

I bit the inside of my cheek to keep from laughing.

"I've been doing this for a long time. I can manage on my own, thank you." He peered at me. "Should we get on with this interview before I lose the light?"

Lose the light? We were hours away from sunset. I removed my phone from my handbag where I'd made notes of my questions.

"Okay, Mr. York. Let's begin."

CHAPTER THREE

THAT EVENING, Alec came over after Marley went to bed. He'd been invited for dinner but had declined so that he could finish editing a chapter. Even now as I sat at the dining table and tried to make sense of Ivy Rose's Book of Shadows, the vampire sat across from me with his laptop open.

"And how is Marley getting on at the academy?" he asked, his eyes still on the screen. Once Marley came into her magic, she transferred to attend the prestigious Black Hat Academy with the other witches and wizards of Starry Hollow.

"Okay, I guess. She doesn't talk to me as much about school as she used to."

His gaze flicked to me. "You don't worry that signals an issue?"

"No, I think that signals a young woman who is gaining independence and needs her privacy." I scanned another page of the book and tried to make sense of its contents. I'd thought that once I cracked open my ancestor's Book of Shadows that all my questions would be answered, but it only seemed to raise more.

"How is your article on Winston York coming along?" he asked.

"I still need to start writing it." I didn't miss his dissatisfied expression. "What's the matter? I told you that I'm meeting him again in the morning." After showing me a set of tracks and sharing details of his early career, he'd asked me to leave and come back in the morning so that he could get back to work.

"Yes, but you don't need a second meeting in order to start the article."

"It's not like the article is due in the morning. Why does it matter?"

"Because you have a tendency to leave everything to the last minute and then stress yourself unnecessarily." He gestured to the book. "For example, why are you reading for pleasure when you could be completing the first draft?"

A twisted ball of guilt and annoyance solidified in my stomach. "This isn't pleasure. I try to study Ivy's book when Marley's not around. I'm usually too busy during the days so this is my only opportunity."

"Why can't Marley be a part of it? Ivy is her ancestor too."

"Because I don't know what I'm going to find. I told you that some of the stories are distressing. I've had nightmares." Ivy had been a powerful High Priestess who was eventually stripped of her title and her magic. Thanks to Aunt Hyacinth, Marley owned the wand that once belonged to Ivy, as well as the grimoire, and I'd discovered her Book of Shadows buried in the garden. Ivy had been feared for her immense power and eventually cast out of the coven. I didn't think handing it all over to a young girl was such a hot idea.

"Then set it aside and do the work that actually needs to get done. That article won't write itself." I heard the clickety clack of the keys as he continued typing while he lectured me. "I could have easily given the assignment to Bentley, but I assumed you could handle it."

I closed the Book of Shadows with a heavy thud. "I can handle it."

"It doesn't appear to be the case from where I'm sitting."

"And you're sitting where you always sit. In front of the computer. If your face isn't glowing from the light of a screen, I hardly recognize you."

He closed the lid of his laptop and sighed. "Don't deflect. We're talking about you. Perhaps you should consider making a list of all your tasks that need to be completed each day and tick them off as you finish. That might keep you on track."

I stared at him and tried to tamp down my growing irritation. "Look, I'm sorry we can't all be wound as tight as a yo-yo, but I'm doing my best."

"I think if perhaps you prioritized…" A weak sigh of exasperation passed his lips. Those full, sexy lips that I wished were kissing me instead of criticizing me.

"I'm sorry, okay? I have a lot on my plate." I knew I didn't have it as rough as I used to, but that didn't mean everything fell easily into place. I felt pulled in a dozen different directions on any given day and it was overwhelming. "I can start working on the article tonight."

He eyed me curiously. "And when will you do this? After I leave? It will be past midnight."

I rubbed my hands over my face, already feeling tired and cranky. "I'll get it done, Alec. I'm an adult. You don't need to micromanage me."

"I didn't intend for this to interfere with our evening."

"Then maybe you shouldn't have raised the issue. It could've waited until we were actually in the office instead of in my house enjoying each other's company for the first time in a week." Okay, my efforts to leash my irritation had officially failed. "Are you ready to watch the movie?"

Alec kept his focus on the computer screen. "Not quite yet."

"If it's much longer, I'll be ready for bed."

He cut a glance at me. "Then perhaps a movie isn't a wise choice anyway."

"In case you haven't noticed, I'm not a patient lady."

"I'm in the midst of an important chapter and I'd rather not lose my focus."

My jaw tightened. "I think you already have."

"What's that supposed to mean?"

I exhaled. "It means that lately you seem to prefer to live in whatever world you've constructed for yourself. Am I even in it?"

"Very much. I told you I based my main character on someone very much like you."

I spread my arms wide. "How about you spend time with the original and not the duplicate version of me? I'm much more interesting than the two-dimensional one."

"I can assure you that my characters are well-rounded and believable."

I bristled with irritation. "You're missing the point."

He offered a sad smile. "On the contrary. I think I should go now. It's late and I don't believe your mood will improve quickly enough to salvage the evening."

"Oh, sure. It's my fault the evening needs to be salvaged." I crossed my arms. "Go chuckle over your fury book and I'll talk to you when I turn in my interview. On time."

The vampire didn't argue. Wordlessly, he kissed me on the forehead and vacated the cottage. I dropped onto the couch in a huff.

Trouble in paradise, eh? Raoul emerged from the kitchen

with a chicken drumstick and settled on the cushion beside me.

"Not trouble. Just a minor squabble. Happens to the best of couples."

He's not wrong about your scattershot approach to responsibility.

My shoulders tensed. "I don't need another nagging voice in my head right now, thanks." Instead of a Greek chorus, I had Greek critics.

It's not a bad thing to recognize your flaws and try to improve them, is it?

"Not necessarily, but I don't appreciate the way he did it. I've barely seen him lately except at work, so the last thing I need is for him to pick a fight with me." He'd also made excuses to avoid attending couples therapy because of the demands of his new book and I got the sinking feeling that he was reconstructing the walls that I thought I'd broken down.

Methinks you need an accountability coach and it just so happens that I know the perfect someone to help you.

I looked sideways at my raccoon familiar. "First, if that someone is you, forget it. You can't even hold yourself accountable not to eat food from my trashcan. Second, I would never hire anyone who uses the word 'methinks.'"

Raoul gnawed on the meat. *You need a voice of reason. Someone to tell you to put down that slice of pepperoni for breakfast and get dressed so you can get to work on time.*

"It sounds like you want to be my boss. Sorry, friend. I fly solo."

Semi-boss and no, you don't. You work for your boyfriend and your psychotic aunt. You have goals you want to accomplish, but you're too lazy to commit to them. I can help with that.

"And you really think you're the one who can hold my feet to the fire?"

The raccoon shrugged his furry shoulders. *Let's face it. Marley can't be relied on to do it. The kid has a soft spot when it comes to you.*

"Well, I am her mother."

He wrestled a hunk of meat off the bone and chewed. *You don't want to fight with Alec, right? And you don't want to piss off Bentley by doing a worse job than he would. I don't see what you have to lose.*

"I don't see either, but I'm sure it'll become apparent soon enough."

We can prioritize your goals. If you want to focus on health goals first, we can do that. Or personal relationships—that's the one I'd suggest because you're a mess on that front.

My mouth dropped open. "How am I a mess?"

He pointed his drumstick at the front door through which Alec had just fled.

I grunted my despair. "Fine, I'll let you act as my accountability coach and see how it goes. A test run only."

Awesome, so my first suggestion is to brush your teeth.

"It isn't bedtime yet."

I know, but your breath smells like rancid tomatoes. I think that's the real reason your boyfriend left early. He just didn't want to upset you.

"I think you'll find he managed to upset me anyway."

Oh, and I would lay off the dry shampoo. Your hair doesn't seem compatible with it.

I looked at him askance. "Is that even possible? I thought it was for all hair types."

Raoul pulled a face. *I just call 'em like I see 'em.*

I touched my scalp. Dry shampoo had been a game changer, or so I'd thought.

And while we're on the subject, your makeup doesn't complement your skin tone.

"Now you're a Mary Kay consultant?" I zeroed in on the bone in his claws. "Where did that drumstick even come from? We haven't had chicken in a week."

He climbed off the couch with the bone clenched between his teeth. *I can see my work here is done for tonight. Toodles.*

I continued to stew on the sofa for another long minute before climbing the steps to go to bed. In the immortal words of that narcissistic Southern debutante, tomorrow was another day.

I woke up bright and early, determined to start the morning off right. After Marley left for school, I worked on my list of tasks for the day with Raoul watching over my shoulder and offering suggestions.

Work on improving posture, he added.

I didn't even spare him a glance. I kept my focus on the list and wrote—*research recipes for roasted raccoon.*

You realize we're a delicacy in some place, he said.

"Keep annoying me and you'll be one here too." I tucked the list into my handbag so I could add to it throughout the day. I put on my sneakers and ran around the cottage five times. A cramp in my side brought my run to an abrupt halt. I decided to stretch my calves before attempting squats.

You're doing that exercise wrong. Raoul ambled over to examine my movements. *You need to keep your knees from going too far over your toes.*

"How do you know anything about squats?"

You should see what gets thrown away. Do you know how many exercise pamphlets I've seen over the years?

He continued to stare at me and I stopped squatting. "What now?"

Nothing.

My brow lifted. "That judgy expression says otherwise."

*Your clothes are a little tight, especially to work out in. Your body needs to breathe. If you're not losing weight, think about buying bigger. Although if you did that exercise right...*My leg swung out and he ducked before I could make contact. *Don't kill the messenger!*

"Then stop delivering unwanted messages. I need to shower so I can get to the beach on time today in case there's a sighting of the tepid."

Tepen.

"You say potato. I say French fries." I jogged into the house and the raccoon followed. "Are you planning to accompany me to the beach or just hassle me until I leave the cottage?"

I think it might be worth escorting you there to make sure you don't get distracted along the way.

"Distracted by what? A passing squirrel?"

Or a latte that you decide you desperately need. Or a favorite song comes on when you get there and you don't leave the car until it's over.

I frowned. "Those are solid points. Maybe you should come with me."

I'll wait here. Make sure you use actual shampoo this time. You don't want to scare off the tepen.

"Don't eat me out of house and home while I'm getting ready," I called over my shoulder as I hurried up the stairs.

I showered as quickly as I could, but I was vaguely aware of Raoul humming the *Jeopardy* theme song thanks to our telepathic connection.

"Showers are supposed to be my relaxation time," I said, once I was dressed and back downstairs. "I don't need a timer."

If you took shorter showers, you'd have more time to spend on other tasks plus you'd conserve water. It's a win-win.

I was already beginning to regret my decision to let him play coach. I hustled to the car and Raoul made himself comfortable in the passenger seat.

"Don't interfere in any way," I said, as I sped to Balefire Beach. I was unwilling to be chastised by Winston York for a second time.

Maybe he'll be fascinated by me and want to feature me on one of his programs.

I cut him a quick glance. "Is that the animal equivalent of me wanting to be discovered on *America's Got Talent?*"

Discovered for what?

I shrugged. "Pure awesomeness?" I parked the car and we bolted for the beach. When I reached the line of sand, I kicked off my shoes. The threat of grains of sand stuck in my shoes for weeks afterward exceeded the threat of York's steely-eyed reprimand. In the distance, I saw the monster hunter in his trademark white outfit. As I drew closer, I realized that he was swaying. How odd. It wasn't as though a stiff breeze could blow him down, not with that Santa-style stomach.

I ran faster and was rewarded with another stitch in my side. Okay, I was definitely incorporating more exercise into my routine.

"Mr. York, are you all right?" I called.

Looks like he had one Bloody Mary too many, Raoul said.

Winston's body seized and I watched in horror as he slumped to the ground. I rushed forward to see a weird-looking tail disappear into the nearby brush.

The tepen.

My knees hit the sand and I kneeled beside the fallen hunter. "Mr. York?" I shook his shoulders but there was no response. It was then that I noticed his skin and lips were tinged with blue. I checked for breathing and a pulse.

Nothing.

I pushed on his chest. Three compressions.

That's not how you perform CPR.

"Now's not the time, Raoul," I huffed. I bent down to pinch his nose and breathe air into his mouth. I hadn't performed CPR since high school gym class, so it wouldn't surprise me to learn I was doing it wrong. Be that as it may, this was my only shot at saving his life so I was doing whatever I could.

Save your bad breath for Alec. He's gone.

I rested on my heels and pulled out my phone to call for a healer, not that there seemed to be any hope of reviving him. Still, I was relieved when I heard Cephas's voice on the other end. I told the druid what I saw and the steps I took to help. Cephas told me to sit tight and that he was on the way.

As I waited, I noticed Winston's camera set up on a nearby boulder and tossed it into my bag. The last thing Winston would want is for his footage to get stolen and uploaded to the internet by some unscrupulous opportunist.

Robbing graves? Isn't that what you did back in New Jersey?

I gaped at my raccoon familiar. "I repossessed cars."

Close enough.

I held Winston's clammy hand and waited for help to arrive. Cephas swooped onto the beach on the back of a pegasus and his feet slid to the sand.

"That's some ride," I said.

"More efficient in an emergency." His glowing hands set to work on the hunter's body and I knew within seconds that there was nothing more to be done.

"And this is how you found him?" Cephas asked.

"He was standing when I parked but he started to sway

and, by the time I got here, he was on the sand and the tepen had disappeared into the brush."

The druid's head jerked to look at me. "You saw the tepen?"

"The back end of it," I said.

"The stinger?"

"Looks like a rattle, right?" I shuddered.

Cephas observed Winston's unmoving body. "That explains the blue. The tepen must've stung him when he got too close. Its stinger is poisonous."

"I can't believe this. His white whale is what killed him. What are the odds?"

"The tepen isn't a white whale," Cephas said. "It's…"

"No, I know what it is. I was making a reference to a book. *Moby Dick*."

Cephas frowned as he examined the body. "Now isn't the time for a literature discussion, Ember."

"What do we do about the tepen?" I asked. "We can't leave a dangerous creature wandering around town."

"It won't wander," he said. "It'll protect its nest and then…"

I groaned, "I know. I know. It'll return to the sea where it dies like a single mother after her daughter graduates." Poor adult tepen.

He squinted at me. "That wasn't the analogy I was going to make."

"What do we do about the tepen?"

"I'll alert animal control once I remove the body from the beach."

My jaw unhinged. "You can't do that. Animal control isn't equipped to deal with something like this. The tepen is a rare creature on the verge of extinction."

He gave me a pointed look. "Do you have any better suggestions?"

"No, but I'll call Sheriff Nash because he might." He'd also need to inform York's wife.

I hoisted my bag over my shoulder and headed back toward the parking lot with the phone pressed to my ear and Raoul ambling beside me. It was a good thing I didn't write my article last night because today it would have required an entirely new ending.

CHAPTER FOUR

I ENTERED into the office with York's camera tucked safely in my bag and the first thing I noticed was the mess on Bentley's desk. It was covered in worn-looking folders and sheets of paper were scattered across the desk, spilling over onto the floor next to his feet.

"Is this a Marie Kondo thing?" The elf was usually fastidious about the appearance of his desk. Not as anal as Alec, of course, but much neater than I was.

Bentley lifted his head in surprise, as though he hadn't heard me come in. "Oh, hey."

"I've never seen you this engrossed. Is it porn?" I hurried over to look before he could tidy up.

Bentley threw his hands across the desk in a vain effort to block my view. "It isn't porn. I'm a happily married man."

"Plenty of happily married men and women enjoy porn," I said. "Maybe you could write an article about it. Do your own research."

The elf tried to move the folders away from me, which only made me want to see them more.

"Show me what you're working on," I said.

"No."

We stared at each other for a moment like two cowboys with itchy trigger fingers. Without warning, I leaped across the desk and grabbed the top folder. Bentley was stronger than he looked and gripped the folder so that I couldn't open it.

"Show me!"

"It's not your business," he ground out.

I was still sprawled across Bentley's desk when I heard the door open and close.

"Is there a problem?"

I froze at the sound of Alec's smooth voice. I released the folder and slowly slid off the desk.

I cleared my throat. "I'm glad you're here."

"I suppose Bentley is as well. You seemed like you were about to throttle him."

"I have bad news," I said. "Winston York is dead."

Alec balked. "Dead?"

"You might have led with that," Bentley complained. "What happened?"

"The tepen happened. You'll be happy to know that I absconded with the goods though." I wiggled the bag on my desk. "I have his footage."

"Can we backtrack to the dead part?" Bentley asked.

"He was standing one minute and dead on the sand the next. I caught a glimpse of the tepen as it slithered away with its creepy, poisonous tail."

"Incredible," Alec said. "We need to move on our story before the vultures descend. Now would be an excellent time to interview his widow."

I shifted uncomfortably from foot to foot. "Now, as in this moment in time?"

"That is the commonly accepted definition of now, yes."

I hesitated. "She only just found out her husband died. In fact, the sheriff is probably there now. Shouldn't we wait?"

"It's a whole new story now, Ember," Bentley interjected. "You need to pounce while it's fresh."

His comment conjured an image of the tepen pouncing on Winston York. Not a great parallel.

"Can I at least wait until tomorrow?" I asked.

Alec looked at me. "Are you certain this isn't an attempt to push off work until the last minute?"

"No, I'm certain this is my attempt to show some humanity." As a widow, I knew what Winston's wife was probably feeling right now. A reporter on my doorstep would've been greeted with a kick in the crotch.

"Very well then. I have work to do, but let me know how you progress." He strode to his office and I turned to the elf.

"Hey, Bentley, you're a geek. Can you help me with Winston's camera? I want to see if there's footage I can reference in my article."

Bentley begrudgingly vacated his chair to assist me. The moment he was clear of his desk, I dove across it and snatched the folder. My stomach clenched when I noticed the name printed on the tab.

Nash.

Bentley didn't try to stop me this time. Instead, he folded his arms and observed me with an expectant expression. "Now you know why I was hiding it from you."

I opened the folder to see which Nash's information was enclosed. "Who is this?"

"The sheriff's father. When Alec assigned you the article on Winston, I decided to look into cold cases and try to find an interesting story of my own. I think this one qualifies."

I knew that Granger's father had been murdered when he was younger and that the killer had never been caught. In fact, it was the reason he became a sheriff.

35

"Are you sure you want to be poking around in here? It's the sheriff's father, Bentley."

"If there's a story here, don't you think he'd want to know?"

I studied the photo of his father. It was clear where Granger and Wyatt got their handsome looks. I closed the folder and placed it back on the elf's desk.

"Yes, I think he would."

"Don't tell anyone, okay? I want to see what I can dig up quietly, in case there's some kind of conspiracy at work."

"What about Alec?" I asked.

Bentley shook his head. "I haven't told him either. I want to impress him with my investigative skills."

"So that you can supplant me next time there's a Winston York story?"

The elf smiled. "Am I that transparent?"

"You might as well have a billboard strapped to your front with your intentions in flashing hot pink letters." I handed him the camera. "Get your geek on and tee up the footage for me."

Bentley shook his head as he hit a few buttons and turned the screen around so that I could see it. "Yes, that was so challenging," he said, his voice laced with sarcasm.

"An inch higher, please."

Bentley thrust the camera into my hand and I continued to watch the raw footage. York clearly should've employed a cameraman because the shaky screen was nauseating.

"Great Goddess of the Moon," I breathed.

Bentley squinted at me. "What?"

I ignored him and sent the sheriff an urgent text. "I don't understand."

"Understand what?" Bentley pressed, getting annoyed.

"Can the tepen spray poison?" I asked.

"No, you have to make contact with the stinger in the tail. Why?"

The door opened and the sheriff poked his head inside. "Hey, Rose. What's the crisis?"

"That was fast."

"I was just on my way back to the office when I got your text."

"I have something you need to see."

I heard rustling behind me and turned to see Bentley sweeping everything off his desk in one anxious movement. The sheriff caught sight of him and chuckled.

"Last day on the job, Smith?" he asked.

"No, he's just a slob and Alec told him to clean up or clean out," I replied quickly.

"In that case, I'm surprised you're still allowed to work here." The sheriff winked at me.

I picked up the camera and showed him the screen. "Now watch closely." I replayed the recording and watched the sheriff's face to see if he recognized the problem. He flinched at exactly the right moment.

"Sweet baby Elvis," he breathed.

"Hey, that's my line."

His eyes met mine. "This wasn't an accidental death."

"Afraid not, Sheriff. Looks like this was murder."

"Sounds like you're going to be one busy sheriff. Winston York is an icon. The whole world will demand answers and quickly." Bentley kept one hand on the pile of folders, as though the sheriff might somehow realize that the reports on his father's death lurked underneath.

Sheriff Nash smirked. "Thanks for the added pressure."

"Maybe you two should discuss this somewhere else," Bentley said.

I craned my neck to look at him and noticed the beads of sweat on the elf's forehead. Good thing he wasn't on the receiving end of any interrogations or he'd crack after the first question.

"Want to go for a coffee?" I asked. "I can run through exactly what happened at the beach."

"Sounds good to me." When I grabbed my bag, he looked at me askance. "You're a little lopsided there, Rose. How about I carry it for you? Don't want you getting a hunched back on my account."

For once, I didn't argue.

The sheriff looped the bag over his shoulder and looked at Bentley. "Keep this development to yourself for now, ace."

"Yes, sir."

As we left the office and walked along the sidewalk to the Caffeinated Cauldron, I described what happened on the beach in greater detail.

"You need to take protective measures," I said. "You've got a dead icon and a rare supernatural creature with a baby on board…somewhere."

The sheriff shifted the bag to his other arm. "You know we're not equipped for this, Rose. If I assign Bolan to monster duty, then no one's keeping an eye on the roads or helping me with the murder investigation."

"I'm covering the story for the paper. You know I'll be interviewing everyone that you'd speak to anyway."

"Is that an offer of assistance?"

I didn't miss the hopeful glimmer in his eyes. "You know I'm always willing to help, Sheriff."

He scratched the scruff on his chin. "The deputy won't be happy about babysitting an egg, assuming he can even find it."

We lingered outside the door of the coffee shop.

"I think you need to find it before anyone else does or Starry Hollow will be known as the town where the tepen went extinct. I don't think that's a reputation we want. We're trying to bring in tourism money, but attracting angry protestors isn't the way to go."

He opened the door and motioned for me to go first. "You make a good point. I don't suppose it's relevant that your family has its hooks in the tourism business."

I swatted his arm as we joined the line. "Granger Nash, you take that back. You know perfectly well I'm not motivated by any of that."

He glanced at the spot where my hand hit his arm. "Assaulting a sheriff, Rose? Seems to me you're practically begging to be handcuffed by me."

We stared at each other for what seemed like twenty years. Finally, I broke the silence. "No flirting."

A grin split his face. "But we do it so well."

I lowered my voice so as not to be overheard. "Seriously. It's...not helpful."

"Helpful?" His brow furrowed. "Anything you want to talk about?"

I shook my head. "No. I don't mean it like that. I'm just speaking in general terms." I heaved a frustrated sigh. "Let's focus on the case."

"Suit yourself."

Our turn arrived and we placed our order with the barista. I ordered my latte with a shot of perseverance and I noticed that the sheriff ordered a cup of dandelion tea.

"That's not your usual drink," I said, as he paid.

"No, it's Bolan's influence. His husband brews it fresh at home and he's been sending Bolan in with a thermos every day. It's kind of sweet."

I laughed at the image of the little leprechaun coming to work with a lunchbox and thermos like a child. "I wish someone would pack me food and drink to take to work. The less I need to think, the better."

He chuckled. "Is that your motto for life, Rose?"

"According to my aunt, yes."

The barista handed over our drinks and we wandered to an empty table by the window.

"I'll tell the deputy that I need him to track the tepen and the egg."

"Which one came first, do you think?" I asked.

He sipped his tea. "I'm not going to dignify that with a remark."

"Thank you."

"Although it might make sense to get a resident with better tracking abilities to work with him," I said. "Bolan isn't exactly a master tracker. I mean, think about it. It was York's life's work and he came out of retirement just to catch a glimpse of this sucker."

"What about Wyatt?"

"I don't think a werewolf is our best bet, not for a creature like this one."

"Yeah. I guess if it were that easy, York would've just used a team of shifters to find it."

"Exactly. These creatures are rare for a reason. They know how to hide from everyone and protect themselves." My words made me think of Alec, the way he hid from the world in his fantasies in order to protect himself—but from what? His own thoughts? Memories?

Me?

The sheriff snapped his fingers, regaining my attention. "You have a unicorn," he said.

"Technically Marley has a unicorn, but yes. Is that relevant?"

"Do you know which kind?"

I laughed. "There are kinds?" Other than different colored horns, I had no idea about the different types.

"If yours has a golden horn, then they have special tracking abilities, almost like a sixth sense."

"Unicorns that see dead people? Now that's a show I didn't even know I wanted to watch until now."

"I don't know about ghosts, but I remember reading an article about some rich vampire that used this type of unicorn to root out diamonds."

I smiled. "So basically, the fancy version of a pig snuffling for truffles. Unfortunately, Firefly's horn is silver."

"Too bad."

"To be honest, I'm surprised. I thought for sure Aunt Hyacinth wouldn't be caught dead buying her grandniece a garden-variety unicorn. Only the best for a Rose." I mimicked her haughty tone.

The sheriff grinned. "For once, I would've been glad your aunt is a snob."

"I think the word you're looking for is discerning."

"Nope. Pretty sure it isn't."

"This is a serious bummer." The mental image of the leprechaun riding on the unicorn's back was enough to send me into giggling fits for the rest of the week. Another idea occurred to me. "What about a flying kitten for an aerial search? Bonkers can fly low and is small enough to weave through places that others can't."

He smirked. "Next thing you'll want to know is whether we could use a garbage-sniffing raccoon."

I lit up. "Now that you mention it...Honestly, I think they'd be a great team to assemble for this highly specialized mission."

"Is there any magic that might help?"

"I can ask, but I would think if magic helped that we'd see a team of witches and wizards descending upon Starry Hollow."

He raked a hand through his thick brown hair. "Yeah, you're right. This tepen is a big deal and there are some folks with deep pockets pursuing it."

"Really? I thought it was more of a curiosity."

"It's rare, Ember. That means it's valuable."

"Well, well. Don't you two look cozy?"

I glanced up into the smirking face of Wyatt Nash, Granger's brother and Linnea's ex-husband with the roving eyes and hands.

"We're working, Wyatt. What is it?" the sheriff asked.

"Nothing. Just passing by and saw you in the window. Figured I'd say hello."

"Figured you'd be nosy, more like," his brother said.

"Heard about the dead celebrity," Wyatt said. "Sounds like you've got a problem on your hands with that critter on the loose."

I stifled a laugh at the word 'critter.' The tepen hardly qualified as a critter.

"Everything is under control, but thanks for your concern." Sheriff Nash stared at his brother, waiting for Wyatt to get the hint and leave. He should've known better. Wyatt's contrary nature wouldn't allow him to politely retreat.

"You know, you should really think about changing careers," Wyatt said, his gaze on me. "You spend more time playing the role of his deputy than anything else."

"I'm writing an article on York and the tepen for *Vox Populi*," I said. "And I was there when he died. I'm sharing helpful information."

He snorted. "Yeah, sure. You two making eyes at each other is totally professional in nature."

Sheriff Nash bristled. "Using our power of sight to look at each other isn't the same as 'making eyes' at each other and you know it. Now stop being a pain in the rear and move along."

Wyatt shoved his hands in his pockets. "Suit yourself, brother, but I'd tread carefully if I were you. You lost out to that vamp twice now and I don't know that the third time's the charm."

I knew he was referencing Tatiana, the manipulative fairy that Granger and Alec had pursued years ago who'd since died, and then me.

"Wyatt, the day I heed relationship advice from you is the day I shift into a tadpole." His stubborn jaw was tense. "Mind your business and let us get back to work."

Wyatt swiveled on his heel and swaggered out of the coffee shop, pausing a brief moment to check out an attractive pixie who'd just entered.

"Sorry about that," the sheriff said.

"He's Wyatt. He'll never change."

He leaned against the back of his chair. "No, once you get to a certain age, I think that's pretty much it."

Again, my thoughts turned to Alec. If a paranormal with a normal lifespan was incapable of change, could an immortal vampire possibly change? I brushed the doubts aside. I loved Alec and he deserved my unwavering support.

"Are you going to go back to York's house and tell his wife about the footage?" I asked.

"Not yet. I'd like to keep this quiet for as long as possible or we'll have the international news media on our front stoop. It'll cause too much chaos and disrupt the investigation."

"Then how are you going to investigate and interrogate suspects?"

He gave me a lazy grin. "That's where you come in, Rose."

"I guess Wyatt was right. I'm acting as your deputy yet again."

"My undercover deputy," he corrected me. "Have you spoken to Mabel York yet for your article?"

"No, it's on my to-do list."

"Perfect. Then, if you don't mind, I'd like you to use that

interview as a way of gleaning information so that I don't have to reveal what we know."

I tapped the side of my cup, pondering Wyatt's remarks. "It's not a problem, is it? I mean, I know you've talked about hiring a second deputy, but, until you do, I don't mind helping out."

"I know you don't, Rose, and I appreciate your willingness to get involved. Just ignore my brother. He's a big mouth with bad intentions."

"He has his moments though," I said. To his credit, Wyatt still helped out Linnea with odd jobs at Palmetto House. Although I suspected he was motivated by guilt, the fact that he felt any guilt at all showed that he wasn't bad to the core.

The sheriff blew out a small puff of air. "Yeah, I just wish he had more of 'em, like when we were kids."

"Trust me, there are plenty of times I wish I was a kid again and I don't even have siblings." Especially lately with my seemingly endless pile of responsibilities. The idea of being young again when my time was more or less my own and no one depended on me for anything...I sighed. The appeal of *Freaky Friday* was growing on me by the minute.

The sheriff finished his dandelion tea. "I'll update Bolan. Let me know when you've spoken to Mabel York."

"I'll head over there right now and call you afterward." I swallowed the remainder of my latte, suddenly grateful that I'd chosen the shot of perseverance—I had a feeling I was going to need it.

CHAPTER FIVE

THE YORK HOUSE was situated in a secluded section of the woods on the western side of town. As I rambled along the dirt path, I noticed the automatic lights of the car were illuminated thanks to a thick canopy of branches overhead. It seemed that Winston was serious about becoming a hermit after he retired. No one would casually drop by here unless invited.

I parked between two live oaks, which seemed to be the only available spot for another car. I knocked on the screen door and waited a full minute before knocking again. A white-haired woman ambled to the door wearing a floral dress and an apron. She looked like a 1950's housewife.

"Hi, are you Mabel York?"

"Who wants to know?" She peered at me through the screen door.

"My name is Ember…"

"Ember? What kind of name is that?"

"The kind my parents gave me." I wasn't about to reveal that my birth name was Yarrow. That story was too complicated for an introductory conversation.

She continued to stand behind the screen door, seemingly reluctant to invite me in. "You're not here to tell me you're Winston's secret love child, are you?"

"No. Definitely not."

"Didn't think so. He was always against having children because of his stance on population control."

I shrugged. "At least he's not a hypocrite."

"The other woman then?"

"Excuse me?"

She huffed. "Are you here to tell me you're the other woman?"

My radar pinged. "There was another woman?"

Mabel folded her arms. "You tell me."

I blinked. "Let's start over. I'm Ember Rose, a reporter for the local paper. I'm sorry about your husband."

"Thank you," she said stiffly. "I'm still in a state of shock, I think. I put my apron on to clean out the cat litter box." She shook her head. "I also poured water into the coffee filter instead of in the side compartment."

"Believe me when I say that I know what you're going through."

Mabel looked at me with renewed interest. "You lost your husband?"

"Not recently, but yes."

"You were young."

I offered a rueful smile. "Yes, I was. We have a daughter, Marley. Karl and I didn't have a stance on population control."

Mabel unlatched the screen door and held it open. "Why don't you come inside before the gnats bite you to death? I can see them swarming out there."

I passed through the doorway and paused to check out the foyer. There appeared to be white lace doilies everywhere I looked. Doilies for candlesticks. Doilies for a set of rustic wooden bowls that looked hand-carved.

"Can I get you a drink, Ms. Rose? I promise I corrected my coffee pot error." She untied her apron and hung it on the end of the nearby bannister.

"I just finished a latte so I'm good, thanks." I followed her to an adjacent room with a huge floral sofa and two uphol- stered chairs. The wallpaper was lined with images of bees. In fact, there were bees in one form or another on every available surface. Ceramic bees. A bee mug that read *Bee Yourself*. A cross-stitch with a hive. A pillow decorated with bees that formed the shape of a W—for Winston, presumably.

Mabel settled on the sofa and I perched on the edge of the upholstered chair closest to her. "I have a tin of cookies if you're interested. I made a batch of oatmeal raisin a couple days ago. They're Winston's favorite kind…" She trailed off, unable to continue.

"Is this the bee room?" I asked in an effort to distract her from her grief. She'd cry over the oatmeal cookies later, of course—that was inevitable—but at least she could do it in peace without a reporter present.

Mabel smiled. "You would think. Winston called it the hive. He was a beekeeper once upon a time and we used to receive bee-related items and gifts all the time. When we moved to this house, I told him all the bee items needed to be contained in one room or else we'd be overrun."

"He doesn't keep bees anymore?"

"Oh, not for many years. Once he started traveling for work, he gave them up. I'm allergic to bee stings so we couldn't risk leaving me to care for them."

I choked on my response. "Wait," I said, finding my voice. "Was he already a beekeeper when you married him?"

"No, but he was dedicated to helping bees thrive. They're

so integral to life on our planet. Who was I to stand in his way?"

"Um, his wife. The woman he loved. Couldn't he just start a beekeeping society and encourage others to care for the bees?"

She waved a dismissive hand. "Don't be ridiculous. Winston's work was important. We took safety precautions. There was only one incident."

My eyes rounded. "And you lived to tell the tale?"

"Thankfully." She crossed her ankles and smoothed the wrinkles at the bottom of her dress. "I suppose you'd like information for the obituary."

"To be honest, I'd been planning to write an article on him because of the tepen and coming out of retirement. I'd intended to see you anyway."

Her eyes glistened. "I see."

"It might be therapeutic to talk about him." For the first couple years, I talked about Karl to anyone who would listen. I had no doubt I made people uncomfortable at the time. I remembered making references to Karl to strangers at the deli, to the grocery store cashier, and even to the gas station attendants—in New Jersey, you don't pump your own gas.

"Winston was a good paranormal who had great respect for this world and cared deeply about its creatures and the environment."

I gave her a sympathetic smile. "I appreciate that, Mabel, but I can read that in every article ever written about him. Tell me about him as his wife."

She laughed awkwardly. "We had wonderful conversations. Even though I didn't travel with him, I felt like I'd seen the world and all its wonders. He loved to talk to me about his projects."

"You never traveled with him, not even when you were younger?"

She lowered her gaze. "Oh, goodness no. His trips involved tents and jungles and canteens of water. If I went somewhere, I wanted a nice hotel and fresh linens."

"And where did you go together? Any memorable vacations?" Karl and I had been too young and broke to travel. We talked about it a lot, though. He'd wanted to take me to see the redwood trees in California. I'd even considered sprinkling his ashes there but felt strange about going without him. Thinking back, I realized what a weird time it had been for me.

Mabel's cheeks grew flushed. "We spent our honeymoon in Egypt."

"That's exciting. I've never been out of the country."

"Our hotel had a pool and the food was delicious. So unusual."

"What about the sights?"

She averted her gaze. "Winston caught wind of a rare creature in the Red Sea and was off and running."

I balked. "Are you telling me you spent your honeymoon alone at the hotel waiting for him to hunt down some magical creature?"

"It was fine. He got his footage on the fourth day so we were able to spend the rest of the week together." She smiled dreamily. "Thank you for reminding me. It was a wonderful trip."

"Where else have you visited?"

She splayed her hands on the cushions on either side of her. "Nowhere. We talked about taking anniversary trips but we couldn't seem to fit it into his busy work schedule. I can't complain. We were able to live quite comfortably and I know I'm financially secure even though he's gone."

"Did he have life insurance?" I asked. So much for tactful and sensitive questions.

Mabel laughed. "Do you really think there's an insurance

company that would underwrite someone like Winston? We were lucky he lived as long as he did."

"Yeah, I guess his job was pretty dangerous."

"If it wasn't the creature putting him at risk, it was the location. Icebergs. Jungles. Mountains." She shook her head. "Winston may not have looked like much of a daredevil, but he was."

No insurance claim as a motive then. "And he put money away for retirement?"

"Oh, yes. That was something we both agreed on. The plan was to live comfortably and travel."

"But you haven't gone anywhere this past year."

"No, but we would have eventually. We were settling into a new routine."

I surveyed the room, trying to imagine their life together. "What did he do when he was home with you?"

Her gaze shifted to the bookcase against the far wall. "He was constantly reading or in his workshop. Every book was the chance to learn or make a new discovery."

"I have a voracious bookworm in my house too. My daughter would rather have her nose in a book than do just about anything." Except magic.

"Mark my words. It'll never change." Her sigh was weary and I felt sorry for her, knowing what the next few months would be like. Actually, they'd be worse for Mabel. She'd been married to Winston for decades, whereas I was still young when I lost my husband and we hadn't had the chance to build a solid relationship like the Yorks.

"Tell me about yesterday morning," I said. "You might want to consider writing down the memory so you have it for later." Mabel wasn't exactly a spring chicken. Her memory might start to fade in the next year or so.

She wrapped her hands around her knee. "It was a typical morning except he skipped breakfast because he was too excited to eat." She smiled. "He was so childlike in that way. For the past year, he'd taken a walk by himself every single morning to contemplate the universe."

"Who doesn't spend their morning contemplating the universe? I'd wonder about him if he didn't."

Mabel shot me a quizzical look. "Really? I always thought it was a strange habit."

Okay, so Mabel wasn't fluent in sarcasm. Duly noted.

"Anyway, I asked him to post a letter for me on his way to the beach and that was the last time I saw him." Her expression clouded over. "The last words I ever said to my husband were 'don't forget to put the stamp on or it'll come back.'" Tears began to spill from her eyes. "Can you believe those were my last words to my husband after all these years of marriage? I didn't even tell him I love him."

I fished a clean tissue from my bag and handed it to her. "It's not like you expected it to be the last time." I tried to remember the last words I'd said to Karl before he left for work that fateful day. There was a time that maybe I could've quoted them but not anymore. The realization made me feel guilty. Shouldn't I remember a moment like that?

"I'm sure he knew, Mabel."

"We took each other for granted. That's what happens when you grow a garden and don't tend to it." Her thin lips formed a straight line and she rose to her feet. "Why don't I take you around the house? It might give you a better sense of him."

"If you're sure you're up for it."

"It would do me good to stretch my legs." She made a show of kicking out each foot and rotating her ankle.

"That would be nice, thanks." We exited the living room and entered the farmhouse-style kitchen. "How did you meet him?"

A smile played upon her lips. "At a lecture. We attended

the cocktail party afterward and discovered we're both half fae. We bonded over that and were married a year later."

"Wow. That was fast."

Mabel shrugged. "It was typical in those days." She opened the back door and we crossed into a courtyard where she pointed to a stone building. "That's his workshop. I'm not allowed in there. It's his sanctuary." She put air quotes around the word 'sanctuary.'

Ah, the old paranormal's equivalent of a man cave. I offered a mischievous smile. "You're allowed in there now."

She grunted. "That's all right. I can guess what's in there and it doesn't interest me."

"If you want, I can act as your emotional support animal while you poke around. I have one of those at home so I have experience."

She frowned. "You have an off-limits workshop?"

"No, an emotional support animal." Sort of. "Technically I have two. One's a bossy raccoon and the other is a geriatric dog with high standards."

"I have cats," Mabel said.

"You mentioned that." I glanced around us. "Where are they? I haven't seen them."

"Winston was allergic so they've always stayed in the spare room upstairs."

"They didn't mind?"

"It's a large room and they have the run of it, although they'll probably enjoy their freedom now." She stopped outside the door to the workshop. "You're welcome to look inside, but I think I'll stay out here. It doesn't feel right. Winston didn't want me to go in and I think I should respect his wishes."

I inclined my head toward the workshop. "You'll have to come in here eventually, unless you plan to keep it as a museum."

"Maybe I will. A way of preserving his legacy." She pressed her lips together and I could tell she was struggling to keep a lid on her emotions. "Would you like a drink while you explore? Iced tea?"

"No thanks. I don't trust myself not to spill."

"Alrighty then. I'm going to feed the cats. I'll come back here when I'm done."

My first impression upon opening the door was that the workshop was surprisingly creepy. I expected a dusty library with a well-worn leather sofa and a tasteful rug acquired from a weaver in a remote village. Instead, the airy space reminded me of a combination of a hunting lodge and a witch's cottage. There were stuffed full-sized creatures mounted on the walls like trophies and shelves lined with jars filled with bugs, fragments of enchanted horns, and colorful liquids I didn't recognize and wasn't sure I wanted to. Some jars were labeled with unfamiliar terms like *siduri*, *vasuki*, and *patecatl*. Books were piled high everywhere I turned, including an unsteady tower of them beside the sofa. I could understand why he kept his wife out of his workshop. She'd want to clean and tidy and then he'd never be able to find his jar of magical testicles. I wrinkled my nose in disgust. Winston was looking less like a creature hunter and more like an eccentric pervert. No wonder he excluded his wife from this area of his life. She'd have been mortified by his interests.

I wandered over to the far wall where there were framed articles, all covering Winston's travels and his latest conquest. I laughed at the poster of a white pegasus with its wings spread wide smack in the middle of the framed articles. The poster would have looked more at home on Marley's wall. I moved on to framed photographs of some of the rare and endangered creatures that Winston successfully captured on film—Winston with a horned animal I didn't recognize. Winston with his hand on a younger guy's shoulder and some kind of winged monkey demon. Awards. Certificates. Winston's entire career was encapsulated in this workshop.

"See anything of interest?" Mabel's muffled voice came from outside the door.

"That would be an understatement," I mumbled.

"What's that, dear? I can't hear you."

"I'm good, thanks," I said loudly.

I shifted my attention away from the walls. He didn't seem to use a desk. Instead, there were tables of different sizes throughout the workshop. I spotted one with a coffee mug that read *Not All Who Wander Are Lost*. Seemed fitting. There was still an inch of brown liquid in the cup, which suggested he'd been in here recently. I studied the items on the table to see what he might've been working on before he came out of retirement. Maybe the murder was related.

A partial image of a creature with red glowing eyes peeked at me from beneath the mug. Winston seemed to be using a notecard as a coaster. I shifted the mug aside and picked up the notecard, flipping it open to read the neatly printed handwriting—*Don't even think about it. You're done.*

My breath caught in my throat. A threatening note received right before the murder? I tucked the notecard in my pocket and gave the workshop a final, sweeping glance before leaving.

I found Mabel in the kitchen with two cats winding their way around her legs. She stood at the stovetop stirring the contents of a pot. The scent of basil lingered in the air.

"Find anything good for your article?" she asked.

"He certainly was accomplished." I leaned against the counter beside her. "Did your husband have any enemies, Mrs. York?"

She snorted. "He's built an entire career around tracking

rare supernatural creatures. There've been vocal opponents as well as those who wanted to get to them first for profit or trophies."

"The ones mounted on the wall…" I had to assume she knew about them. It would be hard to sneak a stuffed creature the size of a bear past his wife.

She looked at me sideways. "Oh, Winston didn't kill any of them. He wouldn't dream of it. Sometimes his quest would end in an unhappy discovery. In those situations, he shipped them home to study them later."

"Is that why he has all those jars with fragments and liquids?"

She stopped stirring and set the wooden spoon on the handle of the pot. "Winston was fascinated by all aspects of the creatures he tracked. He tried to extract as much information from an expedition as he could, whether the creature was alive or not."

"Do you know anything about this?" I asked, holding open the notecard so she could read it.

"Oh, yes. Winston showed it to me. That's from Jarek. Winston was more interested in the image on the notecard. He had a soft spot for those hideous red-eyed creatures." She wiped her hands on a kitchen towel and shifted one of the cats with her foot.

"Who's Jarek?"

"Jarek Heidelberg. He's an activist. He disapproved of Winston and was quite vocal about it over the years."

"They knew each other well enough that Jarek didn't even need to sign the note?"

"Flip it over. His name is on the back in the small print."

I turned the notecard over to read the back. Sure enough, there was a paragraph about Jarek and his efforts to protect the rare and magical creatures of this world from interference.

"This came recently?"

She nodded. "Word spread quickly about Winston coming out of retirement."

"Did this come in the mail?"

"No, he slid it under the front door two days ago. I guess he's in town to protest residents interfering with the tepen." She blew out a sad breath. "I suppose he'll think Winston got his just desserts, killed by a creature that he should have left alone."

"That would be a cold way of looking at it." I slid the notecard back into my pocket. "Thank you for letting me look around. I appreciate it."

"I'd like to read the article when you publish it. Will you send me a copy?"

"Of course."

One of the cats meowed, drawing Mabel's sorrowful gaze to the floor. "He promised me he was finished with all this. This was meant to be our time together." Her voice shook as she revealed her true feelings. "If he'd kept his word, this never would've happened. We'd be planning how to spend our twilight years together."

"I'm so sorry, Mrs. York."

She fixed her red-rimmed eyes on me. "Thank you, dear. So am I."

CHAPTER SIX

ON THE WAY home from the York house, I shared what I'd learned with the sheriff.

"No financial motive for the wife," he said, more to himself.

"And plenty of enemies from the sound of it."

"I'll check the local inns to see where Jarek Heidelberg is staying," he said.

"Sounds good. I have an incantation lesson, but I'm happy to help you afterward."

"Hyacinth still has you playing school with the coven?" He sounded amused.

"It's a way to control me and keep my lack of confidence going indefinitely."

He chuckled. "I doubt she wants that. I think she'd be happier to discover that you were talented enough not to need lessons anymore. You're an extension of her, remember? If you suck at magic, then it's a reflection on her."

"Which is why she sort of skips over my existence and focuses on Marley. She knows I'm a lost cause."

"You're not a lost cause, Rose."

"I'm cool with it. Just because I have potential doesn't mean I need to fulfill it. It makes me tired just thinking about it and I'd rather kick back and eat pizza."

I pulled into the driveway of the cottage where Wren was already waiting for me. The attractive Master of Incantation crouched in front of Marley's herb garden and straightened when my car rolled to a stop.

"Are you offering free gardening services?" I asked as I exited the car.

"Just admiring the handiwork. I'm guessing this isn't you." He made a sweeping gesture to indicate the thriving plants.

I joined him at the base of the garden. "What makes you think I'm not responsible for the health of these fine beauties?"

"Because I bet you don't even know their names, let alone how to properly care for them." He watched me with an amused expression as I lamely pointed at the closest herb.

"That's calculus," I said.

Wren smirked. "Calculus is a type of math. You mean calamus."

"See? I was close."

"No, because that's not calamus either. That's burdock."

I turned away from the garden. "These are Marley's herbs. I try not to interfere."

Wren clapped me on the shoulder. "It's okay, Ember. Herbology is tough."

"Is that why we do incantations together?" We started toward the woods behind the cottage.

"We can study herbs if you like."

"No thanks. I'll leave that to Calla and Marley. My knowledge tank is spilling over because I can't contain it all."

We arrived at the clearing and I was relieved that Raoul was nowhere in sight. I wasn't in the mood for accountability suggestions.

"If you don't want to focus on brains today, what about brawn?"

"Brawn?" I echoed. "You want me to lift things like with telekinesis?"

"I was thinking about a strength spell," Wren said.

I contemplated the idea. "That sounds promising. What kind of strength are we talking about? Character? Upper body? Superman?"

"How about lifting the garbage can without pulling your lower back?"

I wagged a finger at him. "You need to stop stalking me, Wren, but I like this idea." My hand dropped to my side. "Wait. You're not suggesting this because you think I'm getting old and fragile, are you?"

He looked at me askance. "What do you mean?"

"I mean that Hazel suggested a chromopathy...Forget it." I shook my arms. "I'm ready. Hit me with all the strength."

"That's probably not a smart move. If I hit you with all my strength, you'll die."

"Then let me hit you with all the strength." I planted my feet shoulder-width apart and prepared to do some damage.

"Why don't I just bounce you around the woods a little bit? That way nobody ends up at the healer's office."

My mouth split. "Does Delphine like it when you toss her around like a tennis ball?"

"What's with the goofy grin? Can't you just ask with a normal face?"

I touched my face. "Lips. Teeth. It feels like a normal smile. Are you sure it's goofy?"

"It's goofy."

I shrugged. "Sorry. I like you. I like Delphine. I'm rooting for this relationship to go the distance."

"Me too. What about you? Are you and Alec going the distance?"

"Why? What have you heard?"

He chuckled. "What makes you think I've heard anything?"

"This is Starry Hollow. The residents have nothing better to do than gossip and buy figurines."

He tossed a branch aside and hefted another one, testing its weight. "I like you. I like…Well, I like you."

I glared at him. "Gee, thanks for your support. What's your problem with Alec?"

"I don't have a problem with the vampire. I just think you deserve better."

My goofy smile faded. "Why would say that? What has Alec ever done to you?"

Wren's expression turned serious. "Nothing. Look, I should have kept my mouth closed. Let's forget it and focus on the strength spell. Here." He tossed the branch to me and I let it fall in front of me without catching it.

"Sorry, I don't want to risk an injury. I have too many tasks on my list and I'm supposed to be checking them off like some kind of witchy Santa."

"I think that's a naughty and nice list, not a task list. See if you can pick up that branch without magic."

I leaned down and grunted as my lower back twinged slightly.

"Bend with your knees," Wren scolded. "No wonder you're worried about injuries if that's how you pick things up."

I lowered myself to the ground and tried to lift the branch but to no avail. I could only raise the top half.

"Okay, let it go and try again, only this time I want you to lift with the spell. Concentrate on your magic."

I closed my eyes and inhaled through my nose. I felt the energy coursing through me, ready to be triggered. My magic seemed more accessible lately rather than like a temperamental toddler that only came out to play when she was in the mood. Either my lessons were finally starting to pay off or Ivy's magic was having an effect on me.

"Now say the magic word and lift," Wren gently urged.

"*Fortis*," I said. I lifted the branch with so much force that it slipped from my hands and went flying through the woods, only stopping when it crashed into the trunk of a giant oak tree.

Wren gaped at me. "Well, what do you know? I think it worked." He grinned at me. "You might want to close your mouth before you catch a mosquito or two. They're not picky about where they bite."

I clamped my mouth closed. "You saw that, right?"

"I did, indeed."

"I'm like the Incredible Hulk but without the horrible skin tone." I jogged in place and rolled my neck, getting ready for the next experiment. "What else can I throw?"

"Slow down, Ember. Let's talk about the spell. How do you feel?"

"Amazing." I'd never been particularly strong. I couldn't even open a jar of mayonnaise without a lot of swearing and banging the lid on the edge of the counter.

"Good. Now what questions should you be asking?"

"I already asked what else I can throw. Is there a better question than that?"

Wren crossed the clearing and placed a hand on each of my shoulders. "Check in with yourself. You said you feel amazing. Do you still feel the magic? Are you able to do this again or has the spell worn off?"

I considered his questions. "I still feel energized. I think the spell is still active."

He released his grip on me. "It's the kind of thing you want to know before you act, right?"

"How long should the spell last? Is it like a coupon—one use only?"

"This one isn't one-use, but there's no set timer on it. The extent of the spell is personal to the user—it depends on you and your magic. That's part of the lesson."

"Part?"

"Well, there's the actual use of the spell and then there's examining how you feel afterward. Are you drained? More energized? Unconscious? If a strength spell knocks you out after you've used it, then it's not a great choice for you."

"Okay, I'm clearly conscious. Now what?"

Wren pointed to a fallen log. "See what you can do there. Just don't hit me with it."

I jogged over to the log and hugged it before lifting it upward. It separated from the ground like I was lifting a pool noodle from the water.

"Great. Put it down and tell me how you feel."

I continued to hold the log. "Can't I throw it?"

"What's with you and throwing things?"

I shrugged. "Jersey rage?"

Wren contemplated me. "Is this because of Alec?"

My brow creased. "No, it's because I grew up there. It's part of the curriculum." I dropped the log and it landed on the forest floor with a heavy thud. "So wait. What's your problem with Alec?"

"I don't have one. I just wish you could see him the way others do."

"Why would I want to see him the way others do? He's my boyfriend. Not theirs."

Wren rubbed the back of his head. "You deserve to be happy and I'm not convinced that Alec Hale is someone who can contribute to that. Someone as isolated as he's been is likely someone who's inherently selfish."

"Or someone who's experienced trauma and retreated

from the world to regroup. I don't hear anyone describing Winston York as selfish and he was a recluse for the past year."

"Emphasis on the past year. York dedicated his life to a cause he believed in. The situations aren't even close."

He made a fair point. Still, I didn't like him attacking Alec. "Let's drop it before it becomes an argument. Now that I have super strength, you won't like me when I'm angry." I flashed a smile to let him know there were no hard feelings.

"Check in with yourself. How do you feel? Still tingling from the spell?"

I focused inward and realized he was right. My whole body tingled from the effects of the spell.

I grabbed Wren by the collar and yanked him toward me. I hoisted the wizard over my shoulder and proceeded to catapult him across the clearing. He landed hard on his side and groaned. It took me a moment to register that I was the reason he was writhing on the ground.

Guilt overtook the magic in my veins and I raced across the clearing to check on him. "Wren, I'm so sorry," I said, crouching beside him. "Is anything broken?"

He twisted to grimace at me. "I can't believe you did that. That was incredible."

"Uh, thanks?"

He rolled to a seated position. "Seriously. Can we do that again?"

I laughed. "Are you serious? I could kill you."

"Exactly. I need to know that you could—that it wasn't a fluke." He pulled himself to a standing position and rolled his neck and shoulders in preparation.

"Are you sure about this?" I asked.

"Yes. I would expect the spell to have worn off by now, but you seem to have retained one hundred percent of its potency."

"Maybe you should sign a waiver first."

He laughed. "Just focus that Jersey rage on me, Ember."

It wasn't hard. I threw him across the clearing without even grunting from the exertion. I stared in wonder at the dirt-covered wizard on the ground.

I did that.

He climbed to his feet and stretched his back. "How?"

"I…I don't know."

Except I did know.

Ivy.

"Have you been taking any potions?" Wren asked.

I decided not to reveal my theory. I couldn't tell anyone in the coven except Marley. Anyone else was too big of a risk. The memory of how a powerful witch like Ivy was treated by the coven was still fresh in my mind. There was no way I trusted anyone enough to share the information and I certainly didn't want it getting back to Aunt Hyacinth. She'd probably tie me down and extract my blood in an effort to access even a tenth of Ivy's power.

"I've been putting a lot more effort into my magic lessons," I said. "Ask Marigold. She and I swapped bodies and she was really impressed that I managed to learn the spell so quickly."

He shook his head. "Well, color me impressed. I know the story of how you ended up here and you've shown flashes of power here and there, but I honestly thought those incidents were the exceptions rather than the norm."

"So you were wrong about me?" I pressed.

"It seems so."

"And if you were wrong about me, you can be wrong about Alec."

Wren rolled his eyes. "We're back to that, are we? I thought we agreed to disagree."

"You said you wish I could see him the way others do, but

who are these others? Aunt Hyacinth thinks very highly of him. Bentley worships him to the point of triggering my gag reflex."

"Your aunt has strange and unattainable standards and Bentley has to worship him or he wouldn't be assigned any decent stories."

"Tanya dotes on him like a mother hen and Marley adores him."

Wren heaved a sigh. "I'm sorry, Ember. I shouldn't have brought it up. Your relationship is none of my business."

"You're right. It isn't. And what other residents think of Alec makes zero difference to me."

Wren continued to look at me in a way that suggested he had more to say on the subject. "You don't seem happy to me, Ember. That's all I want to say. I've been spending time with you since you moved to town, since before you started dating, and, to be honest, there's been a change in your energy and it's not a positive one."

I blinked at him. "A change in my energy? Do you mean recently?" I thought of Ivy's Book of Shadows and wondered whether it was having an effect on my personality as well as my magic.

"No, I mean since you've been romantically involved with Alec Hale."

Anger began to simmer below the surface. Wren must've sensed my mood because he pulled me in for an unexpected hug. "I'm sorry, Ember. I said more than I should have. Honestly, I have nothing against Alec. I didn't mean to upset you."

I patted him on the back before extricating myself. "It's fine, Wren. I know your heart is in the right place." My phone vibrated and I was grateful for the distraction. "Hey, Granger. You found something?"

"Jarek Heidelberg's location. I thought you might want to

interview him for your article, see if you can get a read on him before I make a move."

"I'm happy to do that if we're still keeping the situation under wraps." I was careful not to say 'murder' within earshot of Wren.

"I think that would be best for now. As it turns out, he's staying at Palmetto House, so it should be easy for you to make a nonchalant inquiry."

I laughed. "Yeah, I think I can manage. I'll head over there now and let you know what I find out." I dropped the phone back into my bag to find Wren observing me.

"Duty calls?" Wren asked.

"Afraid so."

"But that was Sheriff Nash, not Alec."

"Correct." I offered no further information.

"Watch yourself, Ember. You're already broken his heart once."

"I'm not breaking anybody's heart. He asked for my help with a confidential matter and I agreed. He's still a friend."

"If you say so."

I gave him a pointed look. "I definitely say so."

The wizard held out his arms. "Do we need to hug it out again?"

"I think we're good," I said, and strode out of the clearing with Wren beside me. It was only when I spared a glance over my shoulder that I noticed a trail of wilted grass behind me.

CHAPTER SEVEN

"Hey, Linnea." I greeted my cousin in the kitchen of Palmetto House, the inn that she owned and operated. She and her teenaged children, Bryn and Hudson, lived downstairs. Linnea managed to disappoint her mother not once, but twice. First, she had the gall to marry a werewolf rather than a member of the coven. Then she had the nerve to divorce him. Divorce wasn't in the Rose vocabulary until Linnea made it so. The only way out of marriage was death and a few of us had the misfortune to experience that option firsthand.

"What a nice surprise." Linnea swept a few wayward strands of white-blond hair off her brow. She was a natural beauty and a natural disaster who resisted the use of magic to solve her problems. I wasn't sure that relying on a loser ex-husband was a way to solve problems either, but I had my own messy life to live.

I sniffed the air. "Something smells delicious."

"I'm trying out a recipe for baked apple crumble. Rick thought it would be a nice change from the all the processed sweets we've been devouring lately." Her hand drifted to her stomach. "I can't say I disagree with him."

"I'm happy to provide my taste-testing services." I climbed onto a stool and joined her at the counter.

Linnea smiled at me. "I'm sure you're not here to scavenge food."

I cocked an eyebrow. "Do you know me at all?" It seemed like ages ago that I'd first met Linnea in the burning apartment that Marley and I had rented back in Maple Shade, New Jersey. If it weren't for my cousins whisking us to Starry Hollow, Marley and I would have died thanks to an angry and vengeful mobster.

She retrieved a pitcher of iced tea from the fridge. "A drink while you wait?"

"Don't mind if I do."

She poured the tea into two tall glasses and slid one across the counter. "What really brings you here?"

"What? Can't a woman visit her cousin without an agenda?"

"Sure she can. When I invite her for dinner or drinks. But she never drops in unannounced unless there's a reason."

I took a swig of the iced tea and was pleased to discover it was brewed to taste with just the right amount of lemon and sugar. Iced tea is one of those beverages that's tricky to get exactly the way I like it, but Linnea and I apparently shared similar taste buds.

"Would you rather I pop in without warning and interrupt your sexy times with Rick while the kids are at school?"

She laughed. "He has a job, you know." The attractive minotaur devoted many hours to the local garden shop he co-owned with a friend.

"How's everything with the two of you?"

"Pretty good. He's wanted to throttle Wyatt a few times this month, but otherwise no issues."

"I think we've all wanted to throttle Wyatt a few times this month whether we were married to him or not."

She took a thoughtful sip of iced tea. "The kids asked if we're getting married."

"Probably a natural question. You're obviously good together and very much in love."

"Yes, but they asked Rick. In front of me."

I stifled a laugh. "Oops. They're Roses, Linnea. The family isn't known for holding their tongues."

"I'd never seen Rick thrown off-guard before. He looked like a minotaur in headlights." She laughed at the memory. "I thrust an ice cream cone into each of the kids' hands and told them to go play video games."

"Wow. Ice cream and video games? You were pretty desperate to get rid of them. What did Rick say afterward?"

"Nothing," she admitted. "I changed the subject and he didn't try to pursue it."

"And how did that make you feel?"

Linnea leaned her elbows on the island. "Is it possible to feel both disappointed and relieved?"

"You don't want to marry him?"

"Not today. I'm not ready for round two of married life. I'd rather spend this time focused on getting the kids through school and improving Palmetto House."

"Do you think Rick senses that? Maybe that's why he didn't pursue it?"

"It's possible. He's an intuitive guy. It's one of the qualities I like about him. Sometimes he understands me better than I understand myself."

For a moment, I reflected on my relationship with Alec. Did he understand me that wholly and completely and, if not, did I mind?

"You didn't come here to ask me whether I was getting married again, so what's up?"

"Okay, fine. You're right. I have an agenda. I need to talk to one of your guests."

"Well, I only have one, so that should make the process of elimination pretty simply. Jarek Heidelberg?"

"That's the guy." I sucked down more iced tea. "Is he here now?"

"No, but he'll be back any moment according to his last text."

I frowned. "He texts you?"

"I told him to let me know when he'd be back so I could have food ready. He's tracking that creature that Florian is so excited about."

"The tepen."

She snapped her fingers. "That's the one."

"Are you sure he's tracking it?" I was under the impression that Jarek would want to prevent others from tracking it, rather than hunting down the tepen himself.

"I'm not sure. I sort of zoned out after he started talking about the environmental impact of tepen urine on local flora and fauna." She grimaced. "He's a smart guy, but not the best conversationalist at mealtimes. Of course, Hudson couldn't get enough."

"Do you happen to remember if Jarek was here yesterday morning?"

Linnea pursed her lips, deliberating. "No. He left before sunrise, same as today. He said the evidence suggests that the tepen is more active at dawn and dusk."

I turned my head at the sound of the front door opening and closing. "I guess that's him." I slid off the stool. "Mind if I intercept him?"

"Be my guest." She smiled. "Well, technically *he's* my guest, but whatever. Do your duty."

I zipped through the dining room and into the foyer before he could head upstairs to his room. Following a strange guy to his room *might* send the wrong signal. I learned that one the hard way.

"Excuse me. Are you Jarek?"

He paused mid-step and looked at me. "That's right." His floppy brown hair dipped over one eye as though he'd failed to heed his mother's advice that it was time for a haircut. Never mind that he looked at least thirty years old. That collared shirt and sweater vest screamed mama's boy.

I broke into a smile to put him at ease. "Hi. I'm Ember Rose, a reporter for *Vox Populi*. It's the weekly paper here in Starry Hollow. I was hoping to ask you a few questions for an article I'm writing."

His face registered pleasant surprise. "You want to interview me? This is a first. Normally the media elbows me out of the way so they can get a better shot of whatever creature I'm trying to protect."

"I'm definitely not here to elbow you." I flapped my elbows in a show of good faith. "I have questions about Winston York and the tepen."

His expression turned solemn. "I suppose you've heard the news. A terrible tragedy, albeit unsurprising. You can't expect nature to treat you as a friend when you've treated nature with such blatant disrespect."

"I guess you're relieved that he's gone. You seem to have strong objections about Mr. York's livelihood."

He splayed a hand against his sweater-vested chest. "I'm a tree nymph, Ms. Rose. I don't wish living creatures ill will for any reason."

The guy was a literal tree hugger. Well, that made sense. "Are you thirsty? Linnea has homemade iced tea in the kitchen. We can sit outside and talk."

"That would be very nice. I much prefer the outdoors."

No surprise there. Jarek and I entered the kitchen where

Linnea was in the process of removing the baked apple crumble from the oven.

"Oh, how heavenly," Jarek said, immediately fixated on the dessert. I couldn't blame him; it looked mouthwateringly good and I didn't typically go for fruit masquerading as dessert.

"I'm testing the recipe, so it might be awful, but you're welcome to try a piece." Linnea pulled two plates from the cabinet.

"I'll be a willing test subject, for sure," Jarek said.

I made myself useful and poured the iced tea. "Jarek and I are going to sit on the back patio and talk." The more I buttered him up now, the faster the answers would slide off his tongue. Hopefully.

"I can bring these plates outside once it cools," Linnea offered.

I handed a glass to Jarek and motioned for him to follow me out the back door.

"She's a wonderful innkeeper," Jarek said as we settled on opposite sides of the round wrought iron table. "Very attentive."

"She's a wonderful everything," I said.

"I thought she was a witch, yet she doesn't seem to use her magic much." He swallowed a mouthful of iced tea. "It's rare to meet a magic user that doesn't like to flaunt it."

"She's a Rose," I said. "We have a unique history when it comes to magic."

His brow lifted. "Oh? I'm interested in hearing more. The natural world fascinates me."

I laughed. "We're talking about magic, Jarek. There's nothing natural about that."

"On the contrary. Magic to a witch is like salt to the ocean. A necessary and natural element."

I hadn't thought about it like that before. "I guess the

whole concept is still relatively new to me. Maybe I'd see it your way if I'd had magic from birth."

Jarek nearly spat out his iced tea. "What do you mean?"

I waved a dismissive hand. "Oh, don't get your branches in a knot. I'm a witch. I just didn't know it until...It's a long story and I need to interview you, not the other way around."

The back door opened and Linnea eased her way out with a plate in each hand. She set the dishes in front of us and pulled cutlery from her pocket.

"I need honest feedback," she said. "If it's lacking, I don't want to serve it to my guests." She looked at Jarek and her brow furrowed. "Present company excluded."

"I volunteer as tribute," I said and stuffed a generous piece in my mouth before anyone could say another word. Linnea watched me carefully for any sign of dismay. I had a terrible poker face, so I was grateful that the crumble was, in fact, amazing.

"And you didn't use any magic to make this?" Jarek asked, seeming suitably impressed. He'd also dug right in.

"No. The recipe belongs to my boyfriend's mother so I wanted to make sure I followed it to the letter."

Jarek flinched at the mention of a boyfriend and I felt a pang of sympathy for him. He seemed like a decent nymph, but didn't he realize that Linnea was way out of his league?

Heat rushed to my cheeks as I realized what I'd just thought. Out of his league? What did that even mean? Was I turning into Aunt Hyacinth?

"Is it too hot?" Linnea asked, the lines in her brow deepening. "Your cheeks are bright pink."

"No, it's perfect," I said. "Must be the sun. I spent a lot of time outside today."

As Linnea returned to the house with a relieved smile, I downed the iced tea and returned to the crumble for another delicious bite.

"A fellow nature lover then," Jarek said. "There's nothing better than the great outdoors. That's why we have a duty to protect nature from ourselves. If we don't, then who will?"

"Tell me about your job," I said. "You run around the world making trouble? I have to admit, I'm on board with the concept." I shoveled more crumble into my mouth and let it melt on my tongue.

"I'm an activist, Ms. Rose. I don't run around for the purpose of causing trouble. My focus is on protecting and preserving rare species like the tepen. Sometimes I peacefully protest with signs that symbolize my discontent. Sometimes I go a step further and block entrances or slash tires."

"Basically you're the nature activist equivalent of an angry ex-girlfriend."

He didn't crack a smile. "I was fortunate enough to grow up with more money than I'll ever need, so it feels right to spend my time doing something worthwhile."

"How do your parents feel about your job?" I wondered if they were like Aunt Hyacinth who would be mortified if Florian took any extreme action that sullied the Rose name.

"They would prefer that I settle down and get married, have a few children, drive a Honda SUV. That life doesn't suit me though."

"Are you against having children?"

"Like Winston York, I'm a proponent of population control. One of the beliefs we had in common."

"How did you know to come to Starry Hollow?" I asked. "Winston lived here, so it makes sense that he heard the news about the tepen before anyone else. How did you learn about it?"

Jarek ducked his head. "I follow certain outlets outside mainstream media. There was an alert that mentioned York was emerging from retirement. I knew that meant a sighting of some kind." He swigged his iced tea. "I was ecstatic when I learned it was because of a tepen spotting. A tepen is rarer than the Loch Ness monster."

"Wait. Nessie lives?" I'd always thought the swimming Scottish dinosaur was a myth. Somehow moving to the paranormal town of Starry Hollow didn't change my perception.

"Oh, Nessie lives. Multiples Nessies, actually. Beautiful creatures with the most elegant necks you've ever seen." He sighed dreamily. "I only wish that places wouldn't try to capitalize on their existence for the sake of a profit. It puts their very survival at risk."

I thought of Florian and his T-shirts and knew what Jarek's opinion would be of my cousin's attempt to capitalize on the tepen.

"How did you become an activist?" I asked, genuinely intrigued. It wouldn't surprise me to learn his parents were accountants.

"When I was growing up, I was obsessed with nature. Some children made houses with toy logs or blocks. I made houses outside with sticks and invited the insects to live there." He smiled at the memory. "Anyway, when I was seven, I watched a series about supernatural creatures on the verge of extinction and I knew they would be my calling."

"It seems to me that your interests were aligned with Winston York's rather than at odds."

He blew a raspberry. "Nonsense. Winston York brought unnecessary attention to these rare and wondrous creatures. Every time he put a spotlight on one of them, they became more endangered than they were the day before. Same goes for the tepen."

"So you came here to what?" I prompted.

"I came here to do what I always do. Disrupt his filming and prevent him from showing footage of the creature. That tepen deserves to spawn in peace. That egg deserves to hatch without an audience. Thanks to Winston York, there's a parade of paranormals in town and they all pose a threat to the tepen."

"Without paranormals like York introducing these endangered creatures to the world, there'd be little to no funding to protect them," I said. "His films generate interest. Arguably, the film you saw as a child generated *your* interest in saving them."

Jarek leaned forward, his face hardening. "Winston York was motived by selfishness and don't let anyone tell you differently."

"Is that why you left the notecard for him?"

He flinched. "You know about that?"

"I went to visit his widow and found it in his workshop."

"I was hoping to dissuade him. Perhaps if I had, he'd still be alive."

"Yes, his widow had similar feelings on the subject."

"See? Selfish," Jarek said. "His own wife preferred that he stay at home and leave the tepen be, but he was too driven by self-interest to care."

"How is it self-interest? He didn't capture these creatures and sell them. He didn't force them into captivity and reproduction. He didn't have a zoo. How was he selfish?"

"He should have left them alone." Jarek crossed his arms and jutted out his chin. "As far as I'm concerned, he's no better than Lionel Lattimer."

"Who's that?"

"Boy, I really am giving you an education today, aren't I?"

"No need to rub it in. I told you I didn't grow up in this world. I'd never heard of Winston York until a couple days ago."

Jarek studied me with a gleam in his eye. "To live in a world where no one's heard of Winston York. Fascinating."

"No, Jarek. Not fascinating. I'm not one of your rare and endangered species. I'm just a witch." I scraped the remnants of the crumble off my plate and ate them. "Now who's Lenny Lassiter?"

"Lionel Lattimer." Jarek scowled at the mention of his name. "He owns a cosmetics company called Simply Sparkles. Fairies in particular flock to his products."

"Fairies would flock to a toddler's finger-painting as long as it sparkled."

He chuckled. "You've caught on quickly for someone new to the paranormal world."

I wiggled my phone in my hand. "Being a reporter has forced me to learn." I omitted the part about my impatient aunt and the coven lessons.

"Why is the owner of a cosmetics company relevant?"

"You have cosmetics companies in the human world, Ms. Rose. What are the issues that arise?"

I pondered the question. "Animal testing?"

"Not just testing on animals. Someone like Lattimer will pursue the same rare creatures as Winston York in an effort to extract any substances that might enhance his products."

"Wow. He chases down these creatures so he can take from them?" In my mind, Lionel Lattimer and Winston York were nothing alike.

"He's a scourge on this earth."

"Did you see York this week or was your only interaction the notecard you left for him?"

"I saw him once, the day before he died. He was setting up his camera on the beach and I asked if he received my note-card and tried to convince him to go back into retirement."

"I'm sure that went well."

He snorted. "He saw me coming and got out his pepper spray."

"Have you assaulted him before?"

Jarek hesitated. "Define assault."

"Pretty sure there's a legal definition."

He shifted uncomfortably. "I didn't intend to hurt him. I was only trying to protect the nest."

Oh, wow. Jarek had a history of attacking the victim? This didn't bode well.

"When was this?"

"A few years ago in a town called Siren Lake. He was filming a rare supernatural bird."

"And that was a problem?"

His nostrils flared. "Yes, it was a problem. His filming disrupted the nesting habits of the bird. Of three eggs, only one ended up hatching."

"And you blamed York?"

"Of course I did. It was his interference. He should've left well enough alone. The knowledge that these creatures are out there and continuing to exist should be sufficient. No need to capture their images and habits at close range for the world to witness. How would you like to live in a fishbowl, Ms. Rose?"

"Trust me. I'm in touch with that emotion. How did you assault him?"

"I knocked him out of a tree," Jarek mumbled.

"How? You climbed up and pushed him?"

"No, nothing as violent as that. I was trying to encourage him to come down and leave the nest and my powers took hold."

"Your tree nymph powers?" *Most boring superpower ever.*

"Yes, the tree began to shake and before I knew it, Winston was on the ground in front of me. He broke his arm."

"I see." I made a note to check out Winston's medical records and confirm the break.

"Not long afterward, he announced his retirement. He didn't retire right away, mind you. It was more of a publicity stunt to bring attention to his films."

"What happened when he showed you the pepper spray? Did you leave?"

"I did, but I left a message in the sand made out of seashells."

"What did it say"?"

"Go home." He hesitated. "Well, apparently it ended up saying 'go me' because some opportunistic children ran off with a few of the shells." He scowled. "Another argument in favor of population control."

Good thing he wasn't staying with Aster instead of Linnea. One day with the twins and Jarek's activism would undoubtedly turn violent—if it hadn't already.

"If you're interested in a more well-rounded view of Winston's life, you should talk to Lionel Lattimer. He and Winston had several run-ins over the years and I know for a fact that he's right here in Starry Hollow. I saw him at the coffee shop the day I arrived."

"The Caffeinated Cauldron?"

"That's the one. They have an excellent organic chai tea latte."

"Nobody has excellent chai tea lattes unless you like the taste of vomit in your coffee."

"Such strong opinions. I admire that."

"I'm from New Jersey. They feed them to us in the water supply. Any idea where I can find this guy?"

"No, but if I had to guess, I'd say check the most expensive hotel in town."

I leaned back against my chair. "Rich and fancy, huh?" I wondered whether Aunt Hyacinth knew him. I'd have to check with Simon, her butler. He knew all her contacts, plus it would help me avoid speaking to my aunt directly. As much as I tended to bulldoze my way through a situation, when it came to my aunt, I often opted for the path of least resistance.

"What are your plans now that Winston is dead? Will you go home?"

"Not while the others are here in pursuit of the tepen. If I can find the nest, I'll do my level best to protect it from interlopers."

"So you're going to protect it from paranormals tracking it by tracking it yourself?" Did he recognize the irony of his plan?

"I understand what you're thinking, Ms. Rose, but it isn't the same. I keep a respectful distance and my only interest is on protecting the creatures that can't protect themselves." He paused. "Although it seems the tepen did a pretty good job. Never agitate a creature with a poisonous stinger, especially one on the verge of reproduction."

"There are times I wouldn't mind having a poisonous stinger." Instead, I had to be content with a sharp tongue. "Do you have any clue where the nest is? I know the deputy is searching too. He's also committed to keeping the area clear of trespassers."

"Not yet, and, even if I did, I won't share it." He stared at his empty plate. "I hope Linnea serves this again after dinner. It's worthy of a repeat performance."

"She'll be glad to hear it." I collected both our plates, preparing to bring them to the kitchen. "Good luck with your search, Jarek. I'll be honest, I'm a pretty good judge of character and, if anyone finds the tepen and its nest, I hope it's you."

He smiled. "From your lips to the tepen's ears."

I grimaced at the thought of my mouth touching the creature's ear. "Can we try an alternate phrase that's less gross?"

"May all your wishes come true?"

I slapped the table. "That'll do."

CHAPTER EIGHT

I'D BARELY MADE it out the door of Palmetto House when I received an incoming text from Aster. I groaned when I saw her request for me to swing by the tourism office. If she asked me to hand sell tepen T-shirts on street corners, I was going to have to put my foot down. Let Florian put his considerable charm to good use for a change; I had enough to do.

I breezed through the tourism building to the back room where Aster's office was located. My cousin sat at the desk reviewing a glossy brochure of the town.

She looked up and smiled as I entered. "That was fast. Did you fly on your broomstick?"

"No, I was at Linnea's."

"Oh, how did her baked apple crumble come out?"

I sat in a plush chair opposite her. "Amazing. I could never do that without magic." To be fair, I wasn't very good at baking even with magic. Something usually backfired.

Aster set down the brochure and pinned her gaze on me. "I have an idea that I'd like to run past you."

"If you want me to operate a kiosk at the beach full of

tepen merchandise, the answer is no." Raoul would be proud of me—recognizing my limits and establishing boundaries.

"No, that's not it, although I love that idea." She picked up her phone and dictated a reminder. "Talk to Florian about tepen-shaped balloons and popsicles."

"What's your idea?" I asked.

Aster pressed her lips together as though afraid to let the words out. "Brace yourself. It's somewhat radical."

I eyed her with trepidation. "This isn't some kind of threesome request, is it? Because as hot as you are, keeping it in the family is not my jam."

Aster's hand fluttered to her chest in a move reminiscent of her mother. "Good Goddess, no. Where would you even get such an idea?"

"Movies," I mumbled. And maybe the dark corners of the interwebs.

"No, this is a business idea, but nothing to do with tourism. I've been thinking about starting my own venture. A line of outbuildings small enough for a standard backyard."

I squinted at her. "You want to run a shed company?"

"Not exactly. It would be a place for a woman to hide when she needs a break from her family."

"That's called the bathroom," I said. Not that I was able to escape from Marley even then. When she was younger, she'd either find a way to bust in and interrupt whatever I was doing or linger outside the door and chatter away until I couldn't take it anymore.

Aster shook her white-blond head. "The twins seem to sense when I'm heading for the bathroom. Besides, I share my bathroom with Sterling. It's certainly not the oasis I'd like it to be."

"So it's a man cave but outside of the house instead of in the basement." I nodded. "Okay, I'm getting a visual."

"I'll offer decorative themes and customization packages.

I'm going to call them Sidhe Sheds. Do you get it? Because 'sidhe' is pronounced the same as 'she.'" Her expression grew dreamy. "I already have the perfect logo in mind with a fairy and a hill."

"I think it sounds like a great idea. What about your mother though? She's pretty particular about what falls under the Rose-Muldoon corporate umbrella."

Aster twitched. "That's the radical part, really. I'd like to do this on my own, without Mother's involvement."

"Oh, wow." That seemed so unlike Aster. She was generally the one to tow the family line and act as the dutiful daughter. She married within the coven as her mother wished. She served on the boards of several family-run charities. Her own venture did, indeed, seem like a radical move.

"What about Sterling? Did he have an opinion?"

She played with the rose charm on her necklace. "I haven't mentioned it yet."

"Have you told anyone aside from me?"

Aster chewed her lip. "Not yet."

I cocked my head. "You ran this idea past me first? Why?" It wasn't like I was some business-savvy scion.

"Because you'll give me honest feedback."

"You don't think your mother would? Because the phrase 'brutally honest' generally conjures up an image of Hyacinth Rose-Muldoon, at least in my mind."

"Mother isn't like that with me," Aster admitted.

"Probably because you've disappointed her the least."

She offered a shy smile. "And I'd like to keep it that way." Her eyes turned hopeful. "So? What do you think?"

"Honestly, I think it's an awesome idea. If you can tap into what these women want—and as the mother of young twins I think you can—then you'll knock it out of the park."

Her exhale was tinged with relief. "I'm so pleased. I'd built it up so much in my mind that I worried I'd constructed a fantasy rather than a solid business plan. It feels good to share it with someone."

I ran an idle hand along the arm of the chair. "Can I ask why you didn't start with Sterling? He's the one with the most business sense." I worried that they were still having issues. It wasn't too long ago that Sterling was spending too many hours at the office and not enough with his family. Thankfully, he and Aster had decided to actively work on their marriage instead of letting it dissolve.

Aster swept her hair off her shoulder. "We have an agreement not to discuss business with each other. When we're home, we're focused on each other and the twins."

"But this is a big deal, starting your own company. Even having the idea..." And she was so excited about it. I felt sorry for her that she felt she couldn't share that enthusiasm with her husband.

"You don't need to worry about us, Ember. Now that I have your feedback, I intend to broach it with him at dinner. We have reservations later this week for just the two of us and, since we'll be out of the house, the conversation won't violate our agreement."

"Who's the lucky babysitter?"

She smiled. "I was hoping Marley would be willing? If not, I have a backup plan. It's a school night, but I promise we won't be late." She laughed softly. "Between work and the twins, neither of us can manage to stay up past nine on a weeknight."

"I'll ask her and let you know." Ackley and Aspen could be a handful, so I'd need to check whether Marley felt up to the challenge.

"Thank you I appreciate it." She paused, looking at me intently.

"Why do I get the feeling there's more?"

"I was wondering how you would feel about working with me on this new venture."

My eyebrows shot up. "You want me to be a part of Sidhe Shed?"

"I thought it would be fun. You're a hard worker and..."

I burst into laughter. "Aster, have you met me? I don't even close my cabinets if they don't shut all the way the first time. Once I'm more than a foot away, I might as well be on Mars. There's no going back."

She hunched forward and stared at me. "You're a single mother who juggles coven lessons thrust upon you by your domineering aunt, family obligations, and a demanding job as a reporter, as well as a relationship. All of those things take work and focus."

"But I don't do any of them well, Aster. For the love of Springsteen, I have a raccoon acting as my accountability coach because I constantly feel like my life is spinning out of control. Don't you want your business to do well?"

She tilted her head. "Do you really believe you don't do any of them well? Ember, look at Marley. That young witch alone is evidence of your hard work and commitment."

I shook my head. "I can't claim credit for Marley. She came fully formed like Athena from Zeus's head."

Aster clasped her hands on the desk. "Listen, I'm not going to convince you if you don't want to believe it. Take some time to consider my offer and let me know. There's no rush."

"Do you think I'd have the time to devote to it? You just named a bunch of obligations I already have."

"If the business took off, I thought maybe you'd give up *Vox Populi*. Working there was Mother's idea, after all, to give you a respectable job."

Although I knew that was true, I'd actually come to like my job there. It gave me a sense of direction and purpose.

"You seem to have given this a lot of thought," I said.

"I have."

I contemplated the offer for a brief moment and remembered my discussion with Raoul about setting realistic goals and sticking to them. As much as I hated to disappoint my cousin, I knew there was no way I would leave *Vox Populi* to start a business, no matter how much I liked the idea.

"I appreciate you thinking of me—I really do—but I can tell you right now that I won't be a good fit and the last thing I'd want to do is let you down."

Disappointment rippled across her beautiful features and I steeled myself against that look. She might be disappointed now, but she'd be more disappointed if I agreed and then couldn't handle the commitment.

"I understand," she said softly.

"You should still talk to Sterling," I encouraged. "He might suggest a partner. He knows a lot of business-minded paranormals."

She managed a smile. "You're right. My husband is an excellent resource."

I stood and stretched. The chair was more attractive than comfortable. "I'll let you know about Marley babysitting."

"Thank you. You won't mention this to anyone, will you? I'd like to keep it between us for now."

I held up a hand. "I solemnly swear to uphold the oath of secrecy."

A genuine smile emerged and I felt a sense of relief upon seeing it. "I know I can count on you," she said.

"If it isn't Hazel, my wonderful tutor," I said.

The Mistress of Runecraft bustled into the cottage, toting her oversized bag that I was convinced housed a tiny town. She dropped the bag on the floor next to the chair. "Since when am I wonderful?" She squinted at me. "Are you feeling unwell? Not hungover again, are you?"

My hands landed on my hips. "Will you stop implying that I drink too much?"

"I'm not implying." Hazel planted herself in the chair across from me. "I'm saying it pretty plainly."

"I take it back. You're not my wonderful tutor."

"I figured it would be a fleeting sentiment." She leaned down and reached into the bag.

"What are you getting? Are we doing more chromopathy?" Not too long ago we had a lesson on color magic, which is when I made the bracelet for Marigold to relieve her menopause symptoms. I'd enjoyed the lesson more than I'd expected.

Hazel sat up straight and looked at me. "Would you be amenable to that?"

I shrugged. "Sure. It was kind of fun." Anything was better than runecraft. If I had to draw one more stick symbol, I was going to gauge my eye out with an actual stick. On second thought, I'd gauge Hazel's eye out.

She blew a stray red curl out of her eye and lifted a long, black case onto the table. "I'm willing to do anything that holds your interest."

"So next week will be juggling panda bears?"

Hazel ignored me and opened the case filled with a collection of semi-precious stones. "Choose the color you need and we'll go from there. We can make a necklace, bracelet, a ring—even a set of earrings."

"You're not going to recommend a hangover cure again, are you?"

Hazel adjusted a shiny black stone. "I'll let you decide what makes sense for you."

I studied the options, trying to remember which properties the colors corresponded to. "I could use..."

"Ash of pearl in honey?" she prompted.

"Why?"

A maniacal smile blazed across her face. "Cures lunacy."

"In that case, you might want to consider it for yourself." I contemplated the ruby. "This one looks expensive."

"Choose whichever one you want. Hyacinth will cover the cost."

"Of course she will." I tapped the red stone. "What would this ruby do?"

"Wear it as a ring and it cures impotency." She arched an eyebrow. "Perhaps for your nightwalker paramour?"

"That's not an issue, but I appreciate your concern. What about that one?" I pointed to a brilliant green stone similar to the color of Alec's eyes.

"A magic-infused emerald," she said. "It detects and destroys poisons and toxins in the body."

Too bad York didn't have access to one of these, I thought. "Hang on a hot minute. You said it detects poison too?"

"That's right. It changes color when it senses the presence of a poison or toxin."

I stared at the beautiful gemstone. "Can it actually identify the type of poison?" I'd run it over to the sheriff's office right now.

"It's not a computer, Ember. It's a gemstone."

"I'd like this one. Can we make a bracelet with it?"

Are you sure about that?

I craned my neck to see Raoul on his hind legs trying to peer over my shoulder. "What's wrong with it?"

It's a bracelet. You'll lose it in a bowl of spaghetti or on a hand towel in a public restroom.

"That's very specific."

What can I say? I know you.

"But I think a bracelet makes sense."

"Yes," Hazel said. "You and Marigold can wear matching ones."

I glared at her. "I do not need the same bracelet that Marigold has, thank you very much."

Hazel gave me a coy look. "What? You can't be that much younger than she is. You have Marley and she's how old now?"

Sensing a burgeoning crisis, Raoul leaped on top of the table to position his furry body between us. He needn't have bothered. The door burst open and Bonkers swooped into the room and landed face first on the scratching post like she was straight out of a Tom and Jerry cartoon.

"It's times like these I need a YouTube channel," I muttered.

"Bonkers, are you okay?" Marley rushed into the cottage behind her familiar and hurried to check on the winged kitten.

"A stiff breeze will do that," Hazel said.

"I'm not convinced," I said. "Why don't you stand in the doorway and test out your theory?"

The witch tapped the case with prim fingers. "Why don't we stay focused on the lesson?"

"Give me one second. I need to put on my mom hat." I turned to smile at Marley. "How was school?"

She flopped on the couch. "Busy. I feel like I'm being buried alive under a mountain of schoolwork."

"That sounds unpleasant," I said. "Aster asked if you were available to babysit this week. From the sound of it, I'm guessing the answer is no."

She tipped her head back to peer at me upside down from the couch. "I totally would, but I have tests all week and I need to study."

"That's fine. I'll let her know."

Marley's brow creased with concern. "What if she can't find someone else?"

"Don't worry about Aster. She's a grown witch. Besides, she said she has a backup plan."

"If you're sure." Marley seemed unconvinced.

"School is more important," I said firmly. "Set your boundaries and enforce them."

Exactly, Raoul said. He'd crawled onto the chair beside me to admire the gemstones.

No sticky paws, I warned him.

What? You know my thieving days are over.

Explain that to my refrigerator.

Hazel tapped the table. "Ember, could we get back to the lesson, please?"

"Sure. Ooh, wait. Let me send this quick text to Aster before I forget."

Hazel exhaled impatiently. "Far be it for me to interfere with your personal life during my professional time."

A knock at the door interrupted my texting.

Marley ran to open it, revealing Simon with a small crushed velvet pillow.

"Simon, you look like an oversized ring bearer," I said.

"There's a note," Marley said. Before she could pluck it from the pillow, the note opened and Aunt Hyacinth's face appeared in the cottage.

"Your presence is requested at Thornhold for dinner this evening. Seven o'clock sharp."

"But I already have dinner plans," I said. "Those leftover tacos won't reheat themselves." The face dissipated without a response and I blinked at Simon. "Did she get that?"

"No, Miss Ember, but I will be happy to relay your response."

"Oh, about the tacos? No, I guess I'd better just show up."

Is fitting in dinner at Thornhold a realistic goal? Raoul asked.

Her alcohol is more expensive than mine.

Fair enough. Carry on.

"Mom, there's no way I can go to a long dinner at Aunt Hyacinth's," Marley complained. She threw a tortured hand across her forehead to emphasize her distress.

"You have my permission to stay home and study." I turned back to Simon. "Please tell my aunt that Ember, party of one, will be attending."

Simon bowed and vacated the doorstep.

I closed the door and returned to the table.

"Can we please...?" Hazel began.

I held up a finger as I texted Aster to let her know about Marley's heavy workload and my phone immediately rang in response. "Hi. I guess you got my text."

"Is there anyone else you know who could do it?" Aster asked.

I motioned to Hazel that I'd be right back and hurried into the kitchen so that Marley wouldn't overhear my side of the conversation. "I thought you had a backup plan."

"I did, but they've come down with a vomiting bug. Even if they're better by then, I don't want to risk the spread of germs. I don't suppose you could do it."

"I need to keep my schedule flexible so I can finish my article on Winston York on time. There are a few paranormals I still need to talk to." I couldn't tell her about the murder investigation, so I stuck to my usual story. "What about Florian?"

"He has plans every night this week. Linnea's occupied with the inn. Bryn has a paper due on Friday and no way am I asking Hudson. I adore my nephew, but he's not equipped to look after my two."

I drummed my fingers on the island. "What about Artemis?"

"Artemis Haverford? She's ancient."

"I know, but she's great with Marley and she has her own ghost to keep the boys in line. The downside is you'd have to bring them to her. She won't come to you."

"Hmm. Any port in a storm, though, right?"

"Depends on how badly you want this dinner."

I could practically hear her frowning. "I've worked myself up to telling Sterling about my Sidhe Shed idea. I'd hate to bail now."

"I bet she'd be thrilled to have the twins there. Her house is enormous. They can play-and-seek the entire time you're gone."

Aster sighed. "That sounds promising. Thanks, Ember. I'll give her a call."

"Be patient while she comes to the phone. She moves as slowly as you'd expect." I hustled back to Hazel before the witch clobbered me with the Big Book of Scribbles.

"Can we get back to work now or do you have a marching band scheduled to come through in a minute?" she asked.

I arched an eyebrow. "Someone needs a good mood ring." I took my seat across from her. "Why don't we get started on that emerald bracelet?"

Hazel perked up. "Really? You're sure?"

"I am. It'll give me something to show off to my aunt at dinner. Let's weld...or whatever we do."

Raoul sighed. *Don't come crying to me when you lose it.*

I assume you mean the bracelet.

Sure, yeah. Let's go with that.

CHAPTER NINE

I LINGERED in the expansive foyer of Thornhold with a glass of wine in my hand.

"Oh, Ember. Good. You've dressed appropriately tonight." Aunt Hyacinth descended the sweeping staircase with a half-empty cocktail glass in her hand. She wore a floor-length kaftan adorned with cat eyes. No cat heads or bodies—just their eyes.

I glanced down at my green dress that I'd worn to match my new emerald bracelet. "As opposed to?"

"Every other night?" Aunt Hyacinth even managed to shrug elegantly, despite the creepy frock.

"Why are you suddenly concerned with how I look?" I burst into laughter. "Sorry. For a second, I forgot who I was talking to."

My aunt fingered the string of black pearls around her neck. "An old friend will be joining us tonight and I'd like to give him the right impression."

My brow lifted. "An old friend you've seen naked?"

Aunt Hyacinth's stony expression revealed only her

displeasure. "Really, Ember. Must your mind go directly to your familiar's stomping grounds?"

An idea bloomed. "Wait, you said an old friend. Is it Lionel Lattimer, the CEO of a very successful cosmetics company?"

She appeared taken aback. "Why, yes. How did you guess? I've known him for decades."

I sipped my wine and tried to play it cool. This dinner was suddenly looking up. "I'm a big fan of Simply Sparkles."

"You're familiar with his products?" She scrutinized my face. "No. I don't think so."

I pressed the pads of my fingers to my cheeks. "Hey! I only need a light foundation and a swipe of lipstick."

"If you say so." My aunt turned toward Simon as the butler swooped into the room with a tray of fresh drinks like the fleet-footed bartender he was. "Impeccable timing as always."

Simon swapped her empty glass for a full one. Not to be outdone, I slurped down the remainder of my wine to trade it for another one. I wasn't competitive about many things, but alcohol consumption might just be one of them.

My aunt leveled me with a look. "Let's mind our manners for our special guest, shall we?"

I froze with an empty glass in one hand and a full one in the other. "So, no double fisting?"

She turned up her nose and sipped her cocktail. "Simon, where is my wayward son?"

"Your wish has been granted." Florian glided into the room wearing a turquoise T-shirt featuring the tepen curled around an egg. Even in a ridiculous top, my cousin managed to look hot. Some paranormals had all the luck.

Aunt Hyacinth's scowl was unmistakable. "Florian, this is a family dinner. You're not seeing one of your filthy bands in a bar basement."

My head swiveled to my cousin. "Filthy bands? The next time you go to see one of those, will you tell me? It's been ages since the soles of my shoes have been sticky."

My aunt's lips thinned. "I'll refrain from comment."

"That'll be a first," I mumbled.

"We have a guest joining us this evening," she said, her focus back on Florian. "I would've hoped to see you in nicer attire like Ember."

I smiled broadly and squared my shoulders. "Yes, like me. Poster child for appropriateness."

"You wanted me to take a more active role in an organization, so I have," Florian said. "Now you're going to complain that you don't like the way I do it?"

"You're lowering the town's profile with cheap and tacky merchandise," Aunt Hyacinth complained. "You'll end up attracting the wrong kind of tourists."

"The kind with money to spend?" I asked.

"If they're picking up tat like tepen T-shirts, then they don't have *enough* money to spend."

"But you always say money doesn't buy good taste," Florian said. He gestured to his top. "I'm testing your theory."

Aunt Hyacinth huffed and turned to me. "It's too bad Marley couldn't make it. I was hoping to show her off."

"Schoolwork is the priority," I said.

"I think it's excellent that she's so focused on her studies," my aunt said. "The Black Hat Academy is an excellent school, one of the best in the nation, in fact."

"Ah, yes. The best. Whatever that means." I sipped my wine.

"Please, Ember. You know perfectly well there's a hierarchy in all facets of life. That's how the world works."

"Good thing we can bust out our Descendant of the One True Witch card whenever we need to feel superior."

Florian eyed the tray that Simon still held. "Any ale, Simon?"

"Certainly, Master Florian." The butler bowed and retreated to the kitchen.

"No Craig tonight?" I asked. My aunt was currently happily ensconced in a relationship with a wizard. I'd hoped the romance would soften her a bit, but she was the same steely witch I'd come to know and fear.

"Craig is with his sister," Aunt Hyacinth said. "He sends his regards. Aster can't make it either. She and her family already had plans, which is probably just as well. The twins seem to be going through a wild phase. I blame their father."

Of course she did. The doorbell rang and Simon materialized with Florian's ale and continued to the door.

"Why are we the early birds?" I asked. If I'd known I could be late without consequences, I would've spent another ten minutes on the couch doing absolutely nothing.

"Because I assumed you and Florian would be late as you always are, so I gave you an earlier arrival time."

Simon entered the room with a shadowy figure behind him.

"Mr. Lattimer." Simon bowed and made himself scarce.

Lionel Lattimer strode into the room. The vampire was tall and slender with a mustache so bushy, it could qualify as a familiar.

"Lionel, how wonderful to see you. I'm so pleased you let me know you were in town." Aunt Hyacinth held out her hand and he brought it to his lips, careful to avoid his fangs.

"I couldn't possibly come to Starry Hollow and not call on you, dearest Hyacinth."

"You remember my son, Florian."

Lionel regarded him. "You were a lanky teenager the last time I saw you."

"And this lovely young woman is my niece."

I extended a hand. "Ember Rose."

Aunt Hyacinth placed her hand on my arm. "Ember is a reporter for *Vox Populi*."

"How wonderful. And what about you, Florian?" His gaze flicked over the tepen T-shirt.

"He's working tirelessly on behalf of the tourism board," Aunt Hyacinth interjected.

"I should like one of those shirts," Lionel said. "Not such a bright color though. I wouldn't want the tepen to spot me a mile away."

The doorbell rang again, signaling the arrival of Linnea and her kids. I was relieved when my aunt ushered us into the dining room because I was starving.

We took our usual seats with Lionel seated across from me in Marley's chair.

"Tell us, Ember. What are you working on now?" Aunt Hyacinth prompted.

"It started as an article about Winston York's search for the tepen, but it's morphed into a Winston York remembrance piece."

"A real loss for the global community," Lionel said.

"Is the tepen that dangerous?" Hudson asked. "Like should I not be building my fort in the woods right now?"

"I wouldn't be concerned," my aunt said. "From what I've read, unless the creature deems you a threat to itself or its nest, it won't bother you."

"Kind of like you," I said, flashing a mischievous smile at my aunt.

"That tracks with what I've heard," Linnea chimed in. "According to my guest at Palmetto House, the tepen probably felt attacked by York."

I was so intent on the conversation and watching Lionel's reaction to it that I barely heard the voice in my head.

You're holding your cutlery wrong.

I stiffened. *Raoul?*

Who else?

I surveyed the dining room. *Where are you?*

Under the table. I crept in after the appetizers and nobody was the wiser.

I felt a paw tap my foot. *You shouldn't be here. What if Precious gets wind of you?* My aunt's familiar would have a literal hissy fit.

You don't need to worry about that albino hairball.

Raoul, this is a family dinner. You don't need to be here.

Sounds like the ideal opportunity for your accountability coach to shine.

"Ember, could you please pass the potatoes?" Aster asked.

"Sure."

As I reached for the oval dish, Raoul's voice echoed in my head. *Your wrists are weak so use two hands, and whatever you do, don't drop the potatoes.*

Naturally, I dropped them. The dish hit the table and spuds rolled in every direction, including straight off the table and onto Lionel's lap.

"I'm so sorry," I said.

I'll get it, Raoul said.

"No!" The thought of a raccoon paw reaching for Lionel's lap spurred me into action and I ducked my head under the table to stop him.

"Ember Rose, sit up this instant," Aunt Hyacinth said firmly.

"But…" What was I going to say? Please excuse the circus, Aunt Hyacinth, but my woodland accountability coach has positioned himself under the table?

Hudson sniffed the air. "Why do I smell wet dog?"

"Because you're sweaty?" Bryn shot back.

"Takes one to know one," Hudson said.

Linnea gave them a pointed look. "Let's stop now before it escalates."

"Bryn has a boyfriend," Hudson announced. "I saw them kissing by their lockers at school."

"I do not." The pink hue of her cheeks told me that Hudson was telling the truth.

"This isn't appropriate dinner conversation," my aunt said.

"There's nothing appropriate about them," Hudson continued. "You should hear the disgusting sounds they make when they're kissing. Like two animals being experimented on." His eyes rounded and he looked at Lionel. "No offense."

"I don't take offense to that. Testing is a necessary part of our business. If we don't test on a living creature, how can we know whether our product is safe for someone like your mother?"

"So you're prioritizing one life over another," Bryn said.

"Don't we all do that?" Lionel asked smoothly. He'd clearly handled these types of questions many times before. "If your mother and an animal were drowning and you could only save one, you'd choose your mother, wouldn't you?"

"Depends on the day," Bryn muttered.

Uh oh. I could see this conversation heading downhill quickly. "So, Mr. Lattimer, are you in town to see the tepen?"

The vampire smiled broadly. "That's right. I'm hoping to capture it. My preference is the adult, but I'd take the one that hatches in a pinch." He dipped his bread in the remaining gravy on his plate and took a bite.

"You would experiment on a baby of one of the rarest creatures in the world?" Bryn asked. Her contempt was written all over her youthful face.

"As I said, the adult is the priority, but we'll take what we can get." He didn't seem at all bothered by her outrage.

"Do you have any idea how rare the tepen is?" Florian asked.

Lionel looked at him askance. "Of course I do, and that's why I'm here. The value of its secretions is…Well, I can't put a price on it."

Aunt Hyacinth appeared equally unconcerned. "I don't see what everyone is so worked up about. It's Darwinism at work. If these tepens can't get their act together to increase their population size, then it's not our job to do that for them."

"Ah, the old bootstraps argument for a supernatural sea serpent," I said.

Your aunt doesn't like when you make jokes at her expense, especially at her own dinner party with an honored guest.

I'm well aware, thank you.

Just checking, you know, as your accountability coach.

I rolled my eyes, regretting my decision to placate the raccoon.

"My company stands to make millions," Lionel said. "Isn't it far better for me to apprehend the tepen and extract a positive contribution to the world than to simply let it slip back into the sea and die alone?"

"You mean a positive contribution to your bank account," Bryn said.

"The financial incentive aside, I don't see the harm," Lionel continued. "The tepen dies either way."

"But it dies with dignity in the ocean once it knows the next generation is safe," I said. "In your hands, it dies the death of a lab rat."

Lionel fixed me with a condescending stare. "Does a monster need dignity, Ms. Rose?"

"You're a vampire," I shot back. "You tell me."

Zing! Direct hit! Raoul said from under the table.

"Ember," my aunt scolded me. "Please refrain from being

rude to my guest. I would think you of all paranormals would think twice before referring to a vampire as a monster."

"You're right." I straightened in my chair. "I apologize for the remark, but my point stands. A monster, or whatever you want to call the tepen, deserves dignity as much as any living creature."

Lionel ran his cloth napkin along his fangs. "I am quite accustomed to standing on the opposite side of an ethical line. I can assure you that I won't budge on this issue. If this one creature can provide a substance that allows us to help millions of customers, then that outweighs the need for a dignified death in my view."

"Easy for an immortal to say," Bryn huffed.

"I think you and I have different definitions of 'help,'" I said. "I *might* be more willing to consider your point of view if we were talking about an incurable disease, but we're not. We're talking about superficial reasons."

Back away slowly, Raoul advised. *No one is changing anybody else's mind at the dinner table. It's a guaranteed outcome like hitting every red light when you're in a hurry.*

Lionel set down his fork and gave me an appraising look. "You're wearing makeup this evening, are you not? I see a faint shimmer of bronzing powder. A bit of mascara and, of course, lipstick."

I sank against the back of my chair. "It's foundation, not bronzing powder."

"How would you feel if you couldn't wear these products? Old? Haggard?"

"These products are made without sacrificing the life of a creature that deserves better," I argued.

"The dignity, not the life," he reminded me. "Two very different things."

"Unless the tepen escapes you and you take the egg

instead," I said. "You said you'd be willing to do that—take what you can get?"

Annoyance flickered in Lionel's eyes. "I have a responsibility to my customers, Ms. Rose, not to these strange monsters and their supporters."

"I take it you've encountered Winston York before," I said. There was no point in passing up the opportunity to question him about his death.

"Naturally," Lionel said. "It's inevitable that we'd cross paths when you're as dogged as I am in pursuit of the best ingredients."

"I still use that youth serum you sent me years ago," Aunt Hyacinth said. "I buy a new jar every six months like clockwork."

"I can tell," Lionel said, smiling at her. "You practically glow, my dear."

Raoul made a gagging sound.

"Did anyone hear that?" Linnea asked. "It sounds like Precious might be throwing up a hairball somewhere."

"Linnea," my aunt said sternly.

"Have you seen York since your arrival in town?" I asked.

"Ember, this is not the time to quiz our guest." My aunt's warning tone was loud and clear.

"I'm a reporter, remember? You're the one who decided it would be a respectable career for me."

"I don't mind, Hyacinth," Lionel said. "Any press is good press as far as I'm concerned." The vampire speared a potato and popped it into his mouth. "My name in the paper means free publicity for Simply Sparkles."

I wondered if he'd feel that way if he were arrested for murder. Probably not the kind of publicity he had in mind.

Lionel sipped from his goblet. "Hyacinth, I just want to say that this meal is everything I expected from Thornhold and then some. The wine is spectacular."

My aunt beamed as though she'd stomped on the grapes herself. "Why, thank you, Lionel. It's from a vineyard in Shimmering Hills. One of my personal favorites."

"I'm not at all surprised. I visited there myself a few years ago. Now that I'm tasting this, I think I should book another trip."

"What about you, Mother?" Florian asked. "A trip like that might do you good."

She looked down her nose at the wizard. "Do me good? Do I seem in need?"

He shrank back. "No, of course not. I only mean that you enjoy wine and you haven't taken a trip in ages. You and Craig could go together."

Aunt Hyacinth looked at Lionel. "Can you believe this? My own son is trying to get rid of me, probably so he can throw a party in my house."

Florian groaned and sucked down his third glass of ale. "I was only thinking of you."

"I think it's a great idea," Linnea said. "You deserve a getaway."

"A discussion for another time," my aunt said.

"Yes," I said, a little too forcefully. I needed to steer the conversation back to Winston York so I could get Lionel to answer my questions. With a couple glasses of wine in his system, I might have a shot at loosening his tongue. "So did you see Winston York this week, Mr. Lattimer?" Oh well. Subtlety was never my strong suit.

Lionel chuckled. "Like a dog with a bone. An excellent quality in a reporter."

"Forgive her lack of tact, darling," my aunt said. "Some wild beasts cannot be tamed."

"She's from New Jersey," Hudson added.

"Ah, I see." Lionel sliced through his roast beef. "As it happens, I did see Winston and I'm glad of it, given that it was the last chance I'd ever have. Despite our differences, I admired him greatly."

"Where did you see him?" I pressed.

"Balefire Beach the evening before he died," Lionel said.

"What made you decide to go to the beach?" I asked.

"Same reason as Winston. Because that was the best place to begin the search. According to eyewitnesses, the tepen came ashore there so I wanted to look for clues to its current location to pass along to my assistant."

"Did you find any?" Bryn asked.

"Nothing that panned out." Lionel tipped the gravy boat and smothered his remaining beef. "No magic tonight, Hyacinth? I've been waiting on myself, it seems."

"As a vampire, I thought you'd be more comfortable without enhancements," my aunt said.

Wow. Aunt Hyacinth was letting him criticize her hostessing? She must really like his cosmetics.

"What did you and York talk about?" I asked.

"We exchanged the usual pleasantries," Lionel said. "He asked if I intended to disrupt his pursuit of the tepen. I told him that I had no intention of doing so, but that it could very well be a byproduct of pursuing my own interests."

I swallowed a mouthful of potatoes. I was a sucker for buttered carbs. And salted carbs. And sugared carbs. Basically carbs.

"And how did he respond?" I asked.

"As expected. He asked me to leave the area and not to go after the tepen or the egg. It was the same conversation we've had many times before, just swap the last creature we squabbled over for the word 'tepen.'"

"Which creature was that?" Bryn asked.

Aunt Hyacinth looked at her sharply. "Does it matter, dear?"

"I was just curious who won that round," Bryn said.

I had to admit, it was a nice surprise to watch my young cousin blossom before my very eyes. It seemed that rare and endangered supernatural creatures was a button we didn't know we could press.

"If you must know, Winston won that round," Lionel replied. "He always had a knack for ferreting out these monsters. It was his gift. If I could've hired him, I would have."

"Did you try?" I asked.

"Naturally. Several times over the years. He wasn't motivated by money though." Lionel sounded bemused. "In the end, I couldn't find a carrot he was willing to bite. He didn't need anything from me."

"I understand how frustrating that must've been for you," Aunt Hyacinth said. "It's challenging to get the result you want when the usual methods don't apply."

I briefly wondered whether she was referring to my father. When he'd fled Starry Hollow with me after my mother died, it had been to keep me away from the family. To let me grow up outside of the magical world and out from under my aunt's thumb. Sometimes I wondered what my father would think of this—of Marley and I living in Rose Cottage and having weekly dinners at Thornhold. I didn't want to disappoint him. At the same time, I truly felt that coming here had been the positive change we didn't know we needed in our lives. I was a repo agent in a crappy apartment with no sign of improvement. Starry Hollow changed all that for the better. If my aunt's thumb was the price I had to pay for this, then so be it.

"You must have access to all sorts of toxins in your line of work," I said.

"Absolutely. They're an integral part of my business."

"Anything that acts similar to the tepen's poison?" I asked.

He frowned. "Why do you ask?"

"I was just thinking that maybe you don't need the tepen. Maybe you already have a substance that acts similarly enough to the one you're after."

Lionel's polite facade was beginning to show signs of wear and tear. "If you must know, my team already has a product in mind based on the properties we believe the tepen possesses. The fact that my main competitor is in town tells me I'm not the only one to think this. Everyone with brains in this business recognizes the value of the tepen."

"Which competitor?" Aunt Hyacinth asked.

"Amanda M'Leigh from You Glow Girl Cosmetics."

"You've seen her?" I asked.

"Hard to miss the stubborn witch. She travels with an entourage of feline companions."

"Awesome," Hudson said. "When I'm older, I want to travel with an entourage of dogs."

"You will," Aunt Hyacinth sniffed. "They're called your father's family."

Lattimer gave a rueful shake of his head. "Ms. M'Leigh is under the misguided impression that she can get to the tepen before I can."

"And why do you think she can't?" I asked. If he made a sexist comment, he was going to find the ends of his mustache dipped in cyanide.

"Because she lacks my experience. I'm a vampire, my dear. I've been pursuing rare ingredients for my products before that banshee was even in diapers."

Not that I wanted anyone to seize the tepen for financial reasons, but I fully supported this Amanda M'Leigh in her efforts to kick his smug vampire butt—unless, of course, she was responsible for the murder of Winston York.

"You must've been angry when a mere mortal like York seemed poised to outmaneuver you yet again," I said.

"I'm competitive, Ms. Rose, but never angry. My assistant

and I simply carried on with our own search and left him recording."

I latched on to the mention of an assistant. "You were with someone at the beach?"

"Yes, Farley travels everywhere with me. He's small and spry, able to fit in places where I can't. He used to be a petty thief until I convinced him to join my team and earn an honest living."

Hey, the vampire has his own Raoul, the raccoon said.

And yet there's no sign of Farley under the table with you. How did I get so lucky?

"With Winston York out of the way, we have an excellent shot at finding the tepen before anyone else. May the best paranormal win-that's my motto."

"In my experience, the best paranormal usually does," my aunt added.

Two smug elitists. How delightful. Lionel raised the goblet to his lips, his air of superiority fully intact.

"An international icon is dead," I said. "Even if you manage to capture the tepen, trust me, I don't think anybody's coming out a winner this time around."

CHAPTER TEN

THE NEXT MORNING, I awoke to a text from Sheriff Nash asking me to meet him at his office for an update on the investigation. I rolled over and dropped the phone beside me on the bed. I wasn't quite ready to face the day yet. At the base of the bed, PP3 whimpered.

You have a magic lesson this morning, don't forget. You'll need to figure out how to fit in the sheriff without screwing up your other responsibilities, an annoyingly bossy voice said. *Knowing your limitations is part of setting yourself up for a successful day.*

I groaned and wrapped the pillow around my ears. "The only bossy voice I should be hearing in my bedroom at this hour is my own."

Raoul climbed onto the bed, prompting a growl from the territorial Yorkshire terrier.

Marley flung open the bedroom door. "Mom, I can't find my purple cloak and it's spirit day."

"Great, now it's a party." I released the pillow and sat up. "Did you check the pile of clothes on your dresser that you haven't put away?"

Marley's eyes narrowed. "I think you mean the pile of

clothes on your dresser that you haven't given to me to put away?"

I followed her gaze to the top of my dresser where, sure enough, clothes were draped across the top after a half-hearted attempt at folding them. "Oops."

Marley crossed the room and tugged the purple cloak from where it was nestled between multiple articles of clothing. "Thanks, Mom. You're the best."

Boy, her threshold is pretty low.

I flipped back the covers far enough that they settled on the raccoon's head. PP3 leaped from the corner of the bed and followed me to the bathroom. I started to close the door between us so he couldn't follow.

"I don't need an audience, thanks."

Do you want me to respond to the sheriff for you? Raoul asked.

There were far too many ways that could go wrong. *Do not touch my phone,* I warned.

When you say don't touch it, that's the same as permission, right?

Sweet baby Elvis. I bolted from the bathroom and swiped the phone from the raccoon's paws. "Can you even type in English?"

Don't worry. I sent one of those funny pictures.

I scanned the sent text to see whether there was a cause for concern. My eyes popped when I saw what he'd sent. "Raoul, that's not a funny picture. How did you even find that?" The image was a nearly naked woman writhing on the beach. Her back was arched suggestively and she displayed an ample amount of side boob. "He's going to think I'm sexting him!" I closed my eyes and prayed for mercy.

Can't you delete it?

"Not if he's already read it." Which, according to the bottom of the text message, he had. I quickly typed an apology and told him that Raoul had been playing on my phone. I hoped he believed it or it would be one awkward meeting in his office later.

Now that you're texting him, you might as well give him a time.

I gave the trash panda the stink eye as I typed a response. "Happy now?"

I'll let you know at the end of the day when we can fully evaluate.

I returned to the bathroom to shower and change and, this time, the phone came with me. I had just enough time to wolf down breakfast and kiss Marley goodbye before Calla appeared on the doorstep. Although this wasn't a Hyacinth-sanctioned lesson, the crone and former High Priestess had taken pity on me and agreed to help me with Marley's herb garden so that I didn't destroy it. I wanted to show Marley that I cared about the things that were important to her.

"Good morning, Ember." The elderly witch entered the cottage and removed her cloak. She dropped it straight onto Raoul. The raccoon simply took it in stride and dragged the cloak to the coat rack in the corner.

"Thanks for coming," I said. "I appreciate your willingness to help."

"I may no longer be the High Priestess, but I'm happy to serve the coven in any way I can." A shiny barrette in the shape of a flower pinned back her thinning white hair.

"I also appreciate your discretion." I didn't want anyone to know I was getting remedial help with a garden. It was bad enough that I still had a parade of tutors and everyone believed my magic would be eclipsed by my adolescent daughter any day now.

"It's nothing to be ashamed of, you know. It isn't your fault that you didn't grow up in your own skin."

You should offer her a drink.

Are you my accountability coach or my etiquette coach?

I'm holding your manners accountable.

"Would you like a drink, Calla?"

"No, I'd like to get out to this herb garden of yours. Nothing makes me happier than spending time in nature."

"You and Jarek would get along well."

The wrinkles of her brow deepened. "Who's this Jarek? It doesn't sound like a wizard name."

"He's a tree nymph. He's here to protect the tepen from interference."

Calla narrowed her eyes at the mention of the tepen. "Yes, I've heard all about the sighting." She produced a wand and extended it the length of a walking stick. Handy.

I opened the door and gestured for her to go first. "You don't seem impressed," I said.

She blew a raspberry. "A lot of fuss over nothing special, I say. It's the circle of life. I don't see why the tepen needs to be so dramatic about it. Marching into the sea to its doom like its fate is so different from the rest of us. Get a grip."

I laughed at the idea of the tepen as a drama queen.

"You have rare plants right here in this garden that are more interesting than that creature," Calla continued. "Take that one, for example. It has flowers that bloom one day a year. One single day."

"Exactly. Marley works so hard on cultivating these plants. I don't want to be responsible for messing them up and ruining things like that."

"Then perhaps not touching them is the way to go." She sniffed the air. "I can tell you one thing for certain, these herbs don't need to be watered with dog pee."

Ooh. Fair enough. "I'll make an effort to keep PP3 away from this area."

Calla's attention shifted back to me, her expression unreadable.

"What's wrong? Do I smell like dog pee too?" That was a distinct possibility.

The elderly witch scrutinized me. "I sense a change in you."

My hands flew to rest on my hips. "Did Hazel put you up to this? I told that crazed clown that I am too young for menopause."

The white-haired witch continued to examine me. "What have you done?"

"Done?" My mind immediately began sorting through all the things I felt guilty about. I didn't answer the phone last week when Aster called because I didn't feel like listening to ten stories about the twins and their accomplishments. I let the cashier at the grocery store charge me two coins less for the fruit I bought and didn't correct her.

Calla's gaze shifted to the cottage and back to me. She proceeded to walk through the herb garden, hunched over so that she could see each plant.

"Um, are you looking for something in particular?" I asked.

She continued moving from plant to plant. "I want to see if you've accidentally planted something you shouldn't have. Something potent."

"Is that even possible?"

"Have you smoked this one?" She aimed her wand at a thriving green plant with purple spikes.

"I can smoke it?" That was news to me.

She waved her wand back and forth. "No, you shouldn't smoke any of these." She paused and pointed at another plant. "Except maybe that one if you're in the mood to feel groovy."

I made a mental note.

"Is there anything I should get rid of? Anything that's too advanced?" I didn't want Marley to inadvertently hurt herself with any of the herbs. She was still young and learning.

"No, no. All good choices." She looked at me. "Though even the most harmless herb can be dangerous if used the right way."

"You mean incorrectly," I said.

Her cracked lips curved into a gentle smile. "I guess that depends on your intention, doesn't it?"

"I bet you wreaked some havoc when you were younger," I said. Calla had a naughty streak; I just knew it.

"It's the havoc you might wreak that concerns me now." Her mischievous smile faded as she cocked her head, studying me. "Your energy is...different."

A lump formed in my throat. Would she be able to sense Ivy's magic? Maybe it was because we were close to the cottage where my ancestor's possessions were hidden.

Calla tore her gaze away and tapped her walking wand on the ground. Then she walked forward a few paces ad stopped in front of the patch of earth where I'd recovered Ivy's Book of Shadows.

"Nothing grows here," she said. "Yet something was buried." She shoved the end of her stick into the dirt and began to chant.

"Whoa, what are you doing?"

She peered at me. "Helping you with the garden. You don't want to waste this valuable real estate, do you?" She closed her eyes and concentrated.

"Yes, but what are you doing to it?" I asked, trying to tamp down on my nerves. I couldn't let Calla figure out what had been buried here. There was no way she'd keep information like that to herself. As a former High Priestess, she would have a sense of obligation to the coven.

She opened one eye and trained it on me. "There's a spell that can help me determine the issue. Once I know, I can use magic to repair the earth." She closed the eye and started again. "I think the energy I sense is coming from this spot, not from you."

"Weird." I had to distract her. Calla was an old and powerful witch; there was every chance she could figure out what had been buried here. "Do you know of any poisons that could turn someone's lips and skin blue?"

"A substance that deprives the body of oxygen could have such an effect." She tapped her stick on the ground, thinking. "Overexposure to certain metals like silver."

"But the overexposure would happen over a prolonged period, right? Someone wouldn't suddenly turn blue and drop dead. What about any herbs or plants?"

"I've heard of allergic reactions to blue cohosh causing blue lips. And there's a toxin found in Yew trees that can cause blue lips, but I'm not aware of any of those cases involving blue skin."

My phone bleeped to remind me of my meeting with the sheriff. Another of Raoul's suggestions to prevent running around town like a headless chicken.

I clicked off the alarm. "I've got to get to the sheriff's office for a meeting soon, so can we do a quick overview on how I can avoid killing everything within reach?"

"That sounds like a bigger problem than this herb garden." Calla plucked the tip of her wand from the earth and ambled to the front row of the garden. "This one needs extra water. It's growing nicely, but it can quickly take a bad turn if it gets thirsty. You have to take preemptive measures or it loses its potency and eventually dies."

I typed notes on my phone so that I had something to reference later. There was no way I'd remember everything Calla told me.

"This one is called asafetida or devil's dung. Very useful for rituals."

"What does it do?" I gazed at the bundle of yellowish flowers.

"It increases the power of your ritual, that's the main thing it's used for here. Lots of witches shy away from it because of the foul odor, but it's an excellent addition to any witch's supply."

"I guess that's where the name devil's dung comes from." I inhaled deeply. "It smells okay now."

"It only smells when you cut it. It's also good for helping to break free of negative desires, for those that struggle with that sort of thing."

"So it's a weight loss alternative?" I could picture the advertisement—*Don't want to give in to that baked good temptation? Try devil's dung!*

"Depends on the individual and her desire," she said, her gaze moving to the next plant. "The arbutus is a good choice. Protects children."

"We have PP3 for that."

Calla gave the rest of the garden a cursory glance. "I don't think you have anything to worry about, Ember. This garden looks as though it's being tended to by an expert."

"I know, but it's me I'm worried about."

Calla's lips peeled away from her small, square teeth. "Then I suggest you keep a safe distance and let the budding witch do what she does best."

I heaved a sigh. "Fair enough." I'd never had a green thumb, so there was no reason to believe that would change in my thirties.

"Marley is young to be this instinctive. If I didn't know any better, I'd say she was being guided by her ancestors."

My heart skipped a beat. "Excuse me?"

Calla made a sweeping gesture with her wand. "This has the mark of experience. It's possible she's channeling their knowledge without realizing it."

I shuddered. I didn't love the idea of someone as powerful as Ivy working through Marley, even for something as benign as planting an herb garden. If the witch's spirt could do that much, what else was she capable of?

Calla must have noticed my concerned expression. "It's nothing to fear, Ember. Our ancestors are only interested in helping us. One generation guides the next. It's how it's always been."

"You channel your ancestors?"

"Of course. Every time I perform a ritual, I ask for blessings from my ancestors and, one day soon, I'll join them." Calla didn't seem bothered by the statement, whereas the thought made me want to curl into the fetal position and take a long, dreamless nap.

"An ancestor can't..." I trailed off, uncertain I wanted to know the answer to my question.

"Can't what?" Calla prompted.

"An ancestor can't take over a living body, right? Marigold and I were messing around during our lesson and switched bodies. Could that happen with an ancestor?"

"There'd be no body swapping if there's only one body, Ember."

"Good point. What about astral projection though? If I leave my body for that, couldn't a spirit swoop in and lock me out?"

Calla regarded me silently for a moment. "You seem to have a lot on your mind aside from the herb garden. Poisons and body thieves." She chuckled. "Too much time with an attractive author, I'd say."

I cleared my throat. "You're absolutely right. Never mind. I need to head out anyway. The sheriff gets cranky when I'm late."

The elderly witch sighed. "Ah, Sheriff Nash. If only I were a few years younger..."

A few years? Try a century. "He's single, you know," I said with an encouraging smile. "There's still a chance."

"Single isn't the same as available, dear." Calla gave me a knowing look and used her walking stick wand to cross the lumpy ground back to the cottage.

CHAPTER ELEVEN

"YOU ORDERED FOOD?" The aroma of curry and other spices penetrated my nostrils and I salivated at the variety of takeout containers on the table in the conference room of the sheriff's office.

Sheriff Nash was already loading up a plate with poppadum and mango salsa. "I know you, Rose. It's lunchtime. Your stomach will be growling the whole time if you don't get food into it. I don't need the distraction."

I gave him a wry smile. "So this lunch is really for your benefit?"

"Absolutely. I figured we can eat while we discuss the investigation."

"Multitasking with food is one of my specialties." I sat in the chair adjacent to him and contemplated my options. "Ooh, naan bread."

"I avoided garlic for your sake, even though it's my favorite."

"So thoughtful." I piled food onto a plate and opened a bottle of water. "Will Deputy Bolan be joining us?"

"He's not a fan of curry. Besides, right now he's somewhere deep in the woods with a flashlight and a bad attitude."

I laughed. "How much does he hate his life right now?"

The sheriff crunched on a poppadum. "To be honest, I think he's enjoying himself more than he's willing to admit. He gets to frolic in the woods all day and still get paid."

"If there were issues, you'd have already had an earful...I mean, an update. I don't suppose he managed to get one of those teaching unicorns."

He wore a vague smile. "Not really in our budget."

I was curious about the unicorn's unique tracking ability. "What would it have been able to do? Pick up a scent that others miss or maybe magic hooves that can retrace the tepen's steps?"

"From what I read, the horn will light up when she's near the object of the search."

Well, that was disappointing. "I thought you said these unicorns have a sixth sense. Sounds more like a metal detector than an actual tracker."

He cocked an eyebrow. "You don't think it's a sixth sense that a horn lights up when they're near something they can't see?"

I shoveled chicken curry into my mouth and immediately regretted the oversized bite. "Spicy," I choked and reached for the water bottle.

"It's curry, Rose. Did you think it would be sweet?" He set up York's camera so that the screen faced us. "I thought we could review the footage again from beginning to end. See if we missed anything."

"Sounds like a boring way to spend lunch."

"Really? You're not interested in the trials and tribulations of rare and endangered magical species?"

"That's more of a Marley thing."

The sheriff took a bite of curry and regarded me thoughtfully.

"What?"

"Nothing, Rose. I'm just trying to figure out what kind of shows you liked to watch back in the human world."

"I didn't watch a lot of television. I was too busy working or looking after Marley." And sometimes not having enough money to pay a cable bill.

"Is that so different from your life now?"

"I mean, my job and Marley are still my main priorities, but life is easier. Partly it's because Marley's older now and less anxious."

"You still seem to spend your days running through town with your hair on fire."

"Raoul and I are working on that." I dipped the naan bread in the curry sauce and took a healthy bite.

He chuckled. "The raccoon is helping you do what exactly?"

"Manage my time. Hold myself accountable. Develop better strategies for my day."

He shook his head, still laughing. "I like that you're open-minded enough to accept help from a woodland critter, but I'm not sure he's the right fit."

"Raoul is my familiar. Who better to advise me and keep me on track than the animal that can read my mind?"

His gaze lingered on me. "I think you've got more than one option there, but you do you."

My insides warmed and I knew it wasn't from the curry. "What about the report on the cause of death?" I asked in an effort to get us back on track. "Do you have that information yet?"

Sheriff Nash blinked back to reality. "Right. Cause of death." He reached for a file on the opposite side of the table, away from the containers of food. "It was definitely poison, although it's too rare to identify. We don't have a match in our system."

"That fits with the tepen, except we know it wasn't."

"Which means it was another rare poison that's similar to the tepen's."

I leaned my elbow on the table and rested my cheek against the palm of my hand. "I feel like all the suspects will have access to toxins we've never heard of."

"As well as enough knowledge of the tepen to match the two and camouflage what really happened."

"It's lucky York was recording at the time he died or we never would've known he didn't make contact with the tepen. We would've assumed he'd been stung."

The sheriff stared blankly at the frozen screen. "The problem is that I've watched this video multiple times now and at no point does anyone make physical contact with him, so how did the poison get into his system?"

"If we can identify the poison that actually killed him, then maybe that will give us a clue. I mean, how many poisons can there be that replicate the effects of tepen poison?"

"That won't be easy to find. We don't have access to the type of information that guys like York do. We've got to dig for it."

He hit the button to play the recording from the beginning. "Raw footage is as rough as it comes. Watching this makes me appreciate editors."

We watched as York fumbled with the camera and then restarted his introductory monologue multiple times. Once due to beachcombers in the background. A couple times because he tripped over his words.

"You'll see the activist in a minute."

I watched the screen intently. "Jarek?"

"Their interaction is captured on the recording," he said. "I mean, it doesn't show anything that might've happened before or after, but the footage matches Jarek's story."

"I'm not surprised," I said. "The nymph seems like he uses leaves to gently remove ants from the sidewalk."

"True, but sometimes those guys are the worst offenders. Their anger drives them to commit violent acts that they'd never wish on the species they strive to protect."

I laughed when York whipped out the pepper spray and aimed it at the approaching nymph. "York was spry for a portly fellow."

"Years of crawling on the ground and twisting into small spaces will help with that."

I continued to watch the recording and shook my head at one point when the camera fell in the sand. "I know time was of the essence, but he should've taken five minutes to wrangle an assistant."

"Maybe he couldn't get anyone on short notice."

Lionel Lattimer appeared on the screen and I groaned. "I hope it's him."

The sheriff regarded me with interest. "Rooting against the vampire? That doesn't sound like you, Rose."

"It's nothing to do with his species and everything to do with the fact that he's a jerk." Unfortunately, the recording supported the story that Lattimer had told me at dinner.

"Any idea who that is?" Sheriff Nash pointed to a figure hovering in the background, closer to the water. He looked small and spritely.

"Lattimer mentioned an assistant traveling with him. Someone called Farley who used to be a petty thief. I think it might be him. He looks like he has beady eyes."

The sheriff wore an amused expression. "Rose, you can barely see his head, let alone whether his eyes are beady."

"Trust me, they're beady. Call it woman's intuition. It comes from years of dodging guys before they get close enough to make conversation."

"I'll take your word for it." He shifted his attention back to the frozen figure on the screen. "A criminal history makes him worth a conversation, even if you've ruled out Lionel himself."

"Honestly, a guy like Lionel could stand to spend a night or two in jail purely for an attitude adjustment." I scraped the last of the curry off my plate and finished the water. "Thanks for lunch. I wasn't expecting to be fed."

"It's the least I can do. Your time is valuable and you don't have to give me any of it."

I shrugged. "I consider it my civic duty."

His smile faded. "Right. Your duty." He stood and began to clean up the containers. "Any interest in finding this Farley?"

"You want to go together?"

"Sure. Why not? He might have something useful for your article."

I highly doubted it, but I was curious to see what the assistant had to say about his pompous boss. "Any suggestions on how to find him? For all we know, he's somewhere near Bolan in the woods right now."

Sheriff Nash frowned. "I have an idea. Come with me." We left the conference room and entered his office where his fingers flew across the keyboard. "If he has a criminal history, he might have a tracker."

"You mean like a LoJack for ex-cons?"

"I don't know what that is, but sure." He scanned the screen. "Looks like our friend Farley is a spriggan."

"Isn't that a violation of his human rights?"

His brow lifted. "Being a spriggan? It's not like he can help his species."

"No, keeping electronic tabs on criminals after they've served their time."

The sheriff kept his eyes on the screen. "Not human, Rose, remember?"

"Does he have a violent history?" I asked, now wondering how smart it was to be charging after him.

"No, just an extensive record involving theft and minor assault." He smacked his hands on either side of the keyboard. "Got him."

"You can track him right now?" Law enforcement LoJack took stalking to a whole new level.

"Yep. He's not in the woods, which I'm guessing is where he should be right now."

"No? Then where is he?"

His mouth split into a satisfied grin. "How about a nice pint of ale to wash down your curry?"

Sheriff Nash and I parked in the lot of his favorite watering hole, The Wishing Well.

"I wonder if Lattimer knows his assistant is burying himself in beer instead of dirt," I said.

"He wouldn't have access to the tracking device," the sheriff said. "It's for law enforcement use only."

We exited the car and started toward the tavern. "You underestimate Lattimer's reach. He's got money and he's not afraid to use it."

"Sounds like someone else I know. Rhymes with myosin." He shot me a pointed look.

"Myosin? Are you making up words to rhyme with Hyacinth?"

He looked aggrieved as we entered the tavern. "It's not made up. It's the name of the protein in your muscle."

I spotted Farley alone in a booth, nursing a pint. He seemed to sense the presence of law enforcement because he immediately tried to slip out of the booth undetected.

"Too late, friend," Sheriff Nash said, blocking his path.

Farley backed up to his booth and reluctantly returned to

his seat. "I haven't done anything."

We slid into the padded seat across from him. "As it happens, that's one of my questions," I said. "Why haven't you done anything when you're supposed to be tracking the tepen?"

Farley rubbed a thumb along the outside of his glass. "Lionel is a pain in the ass, but I don't think he hired you two to harass me into working."

"We don't work for Lattimer," Sheriff Nash said. He tapped his badge. "I think this speaks for itself."

Farley barked a laugh. "You think he doesn't bribe law enforcement on the regular? He has a whole budget for that."

"And presumably he has a budget for his assistant," I said, "which begs the question—why are you here when the tepen is somewhere out there?"

The spriggan examined us closely. "You swear you don't work for him?"

I held up my hands. "I'm a reporter and, to be honest, I would never work for someone like Lattimer."

Farley's gaze flicked to the sheriff. "And you? What do you care whether I'm tracking the tepen?"

"Got a request to make sure you were staying out of trouble," the sheriff lied smoothly. "Are you?"

The spriggan was quiet a moment, probably deciding whether to come clean. "Fine. I'll confess. I'm playing for both sides."

"No one cares if you're bisexual," I said. "We just want to know why you're in here."

Farley glared at me. "Both sides means that I'm on Lattimer's payroll, but I'm taking money from Jarek Heidelberg to sit this one out."

I slapped a hand on the table. "Are you serious? I love that guy." Who knew someone in a sweater vest could play hardball and win?

"Lattimer thinks you've been out tracking the tepen, but you've been hiding in here?" Sheriff Nash asked.

Farley smirked. "It's a safe spot. I drink ale. Catch up on the latest entertainment news. I gotta tell you, Starry Hollow is a sweet little seaside town. I could see myself retiring here someday, kind of like York."

"You don't worry about getting caught?" I asked.

Farley grimaced. "Lionel would never come within five yards of a place like this. He's too fancy."

"And he just accepts failure each day?" I pressed. Lattimer didn't strike me as someone who liked to lose.

Farley swigged his ale. "I wouldn't say he accepts it, but he knows this is a tough gig. He gives me a hard time and threatens to fire me, but I know he won't. I got too much dirt on him."

My radar pinged. "You have dirt on Lattimer?"

The spriggan fixed his beady eyes on me. "How do you think we met? I burgled his house and got access to some interesting info." Farley's thin lips parted in a smug smile.

"Then why are you working for him instead of black-mailing him?" I asked. "If you have dirt on him, then you should be the one calling the shots, not the other way around."

"Because getting on his payroll was the better long-term plan. I look legit to my parole officer. No one hassles me. It's a nice setup."

"But it *is* legit if you're actually working for him," I said.

He took a long drink of ale. "Does it look like I'm working to you?"

At least this meant there was little chance Lattimer would capture the tepen or the egg, not without the spriggan to explore the more challenging areas. I didn't know much about the tepen, but the thought of the creature in Lattimer's lab made my stomach curdle.

Sheriff Nash folded his hands on the table. "To your knowledge, did Lattimer have any interactions with Winston York other than their brief meeting on the beach?"

Farley eyed us suspiciously. "Why do you care about that?"

"For my article," I said. "I'm trying to get a complete picture of the different players in the tepen game."

Farley drew his sleeve across his mouth to wipe away the ring of ale. "No. Lionel was hoping to avoid him, so I knew he'd be in a foul mood after that beach meetup and he was."

"Why did he hope to avoid York?" I asked.

"Because York is…was an icon and Lionel doesn't want to be seen as on the outs with an international treasure. He cares too much about his brand."

"Did you have any interactions with York?" I asked. Maybe the spriggan got caught trying to snag something that belonged to York and things took a deadly turn.

Farley grunted. "I didn't even get within spitting distance. Thanks to my double paycheck, I'm treating this trip as a vacation."

The sheriff and I exchanged satisfied glances. "Enjoy yourself," I said.

"I'd enjoy myself a lot more with an attractive companion to keep me company."

"That's a sweet offer, Farley, but I'm not on the market."

The spriggan didn't miss a beat. "I wasn't talking to you."

Sheriff Nash cleared his throat. "Thanks for the chat, Farley. Glad that you're keeping things legal, even if the ethics are a little sketchy."

He vacated the booth first and I quickly followed.

"Feel free to check up on me again while I'm in town," Farley called after us. "Anytime. Day or night. You know how to find me."

CHAPTER TWELVE

I SAT in my car outside the sheriff's office, listening to an 80s medley that I'd requested via the magic radio and trying to decide next steps. Sheriff Nash had been called to the scene of a minor fender bender and so I was left alone with my thoughts amidst the upbeat tempo of The Go-Go's. I knew Raoul would disapprove of my attempts to brainstorm while simultaneously getting my 80s groove on, but I didn't care. Music kept me sane in times of stress.

I tapped my fingers on the steering wheel in time to the music, thinking about York and the mysterious poison that killed him. Calla hadn't been able to offer a viable alternative to tepen poison and I doubted the other members of the coven would be more helpful than the herbology expert. I needed to brainstorm. Where could I turn when I needed more information than what I had?

"Aha!" I pulled up my contacts and tapped the screen.

"Starry Hollow Library," a pleasant voice said.

"Hey, Delphine. It's Ember."

"Ember, how are you?"

"Good. I could use a little research help. Are you busy right now?"

"No, as a matter of fact, we just finished story time with a preschool group and I've swept up the last of the crushed crackers."

"Sounds like a real party. I'll be right over."

The library wasn't far, so I took the opportunity to engage in physical exercise and walked over. If I was going to age, I was going to do it with great legs.

Delphine met me at the entrance with a friendly smile. "It's so nice to see you, Ember."

"Same. I see your boyfriend more than you nowadays."

"I know. I'm a little jealous."

"Of him or me?"

She laughed and hooked her arm through mine as she guided me into the library. "What are you working on? Something for *Vox Populi?*"

We stopped at the counter. "Yes, I'd like to see all the books that reference the tepen."

The pretty witch offered a sympathetic smile. "Unfortunately, a few industrious residents have beat you to the best ones, but there are a couple still here that you might find useful."

I fell in step beside her as we walked to the back of the main floor. "I guess everybody has tepen fever now."

"Most of the borrowers were parents checking out the books for their children. Some of them pounce at every learning opportunity."

I wasn't the pouncing type of parent. Marley's education was more of the child-led variety. I watched, impressed, as Delphine went straight to the correct section without hesitation.

"The Dewey decimal system is like your superpower."

"That's only the human world system, but thank you." She

came to a halt mid-row. "Here they are. I'd suggest the book by Zimmer. She's more focused on facts, few that there are. The others are geared more toward the wonder of it all." Delphine smiled. "I suspect you're not here for the wonder."

"Sadly, I don't have the luxury of wondering today."

Delphine tugged the book from the shelf and handed it to me. "Such a shame about Winston York. He was a real treasure."

"Did you know him?" It hadn't occurred to me to ask.

She nodded. "He didn't like to come into the library, but he'd make requests and sometimes one of us would deliver the books to his house on our way home."

"Now that's what I call service."

She clasped her hands in front of her. "I know it's silly, but it made feel like I was part of his research team. Whenever he rang for a book, there was a scuffle as to which one of us would fulfill the request."

I started paging through the book. "Did you like him?"

Delphine bit her lip. "What do you mean?"

"I mean did you find him pleasant or was he a giant wereass?"

She giggled. "He had a gruff demeanor at times. On the whole, I'd say he was pleasant enough. He had an insatiable appetite for knowledge that I appreciated."

"When was the last time you saw him?" I stopped when I reached the chapter on the tepen where there was a full-page illustration of the rare creature. Its hawk head was a mixture of gray and black and its serpentine body was coated in additional flecks of green. Although it wasn't a particularly beautiful specimen, I could see the appeal. The unique tepen couldn't be mistaken for anything else. No wonder the situation here generated such buzz.

"I delivered a book to the house last week, although technically I didn't see him. I left the book on the doorstep."

"Which book?"

"*Rare and Dangerous* by Holden. Winston had his own personal copy, but his wife accidentally spilled tea all over it." She tapped her fingers on a nearby shelf. "That reminds me. I should probably get the book back. I'll wait a week or two though. Give her space."

"Good idea." As a widow myself, I knew the last thing on Mabel York's mind was an overdue library book. It had taken me months to get my head on straight after Karl died. Overdue bills went to collections. I'd been too depressed to answer the phone so there was no chance of getting ensnared in a conversation with one of the collection agents. Honestly, if a well-meaning librarian had shown up at my door asking for a book, I probably would've punched her.

"Do you need anything else?" Delphine asked.

"Do you have any books on rare toxins?"

Delphine's eyes shone with excitement. "As a matter of fact, we have an excellent one, but it's a restricted item."

"Restricted? So I can't look at it?" What was the point?

"Oh, you can view it. You're just not permitted to remove it from the library."

"What's with the restrictions? It's not like the book actually contains the toxins, right?"

She snickered. "No, of course not. Sometimes if a book is rare or old, we require patrons to view it in the Reading Room under a special light to preserve the parchment. It's contactless as well. I set up a spell that turns the pages for you so you don't need to touch them."

My phone vibrated and I looked to see an incoming call from the sheriff. "Good timing, Sheriff. I'm about to fall asleep in a dark room with a book I can't touch. Care to join me?"

"You really know how to tempt a man. I'll be right there."

I laughed. "You don't even know where I am, unless you put one of those trackers on me."

"Then I guess you'll need to enlighten me."

"Library. I'll be the girl with the book."

"She sounds pretty. See you soon."

"The sheriff too?" Delphine frowned. "I thought this was for an article."

"Oh, it is," I said quickly. "The sheriff wants to view the information from a public safety perspective."

"Oh. What is it that you hope to learn?" she asked.

I shrugged. "It's like porn. I'll know it when I see it."

She clutched her invisible pearls. "I wouldn't know anything about that."

And that's why you weren't a good match for Florian. Opposites might attract, but I wasn't sure that dynamic made the best long-term relationship. Wren was a much better boyfriend for someone as sweet as Delphine.

"Why don't we get set up in the Reading Room so you're ready when the sheriff arrives?"

"Sounds good to me," I said. I followed her to a small room a few doors down from her private office.

She switched on the light. "Have a seat and I'll be right back."

I checked text messages while I waited. There were two from Alec, including one with a screenshot of a line from his book that he thought was funny. I laughed, not because it was actually funny, but because he thought it was. I didn't have the heart to tell him the truth so I typed 'LOL' and left it at that.

Delphine returned with a small box and set to work. She pulled out her wand and spelled off the lights, using the glowing tip of her wand to see.

The sheriff poked his head inside. "Hey, Delphine. Rose. I feel like I should've brought a bucket of popcorn."

"No food in the library," Delphine said, panicked.

Sheriff Nash held up his popcorn-free hands. "Just a joke, Delphine."

"Right, of course. Well, it's all set up. Ember, I'll leave the tepen books at the counter for you."

"Thanks, you're the best."

It was only once Delphine left the room that I felt an unexpected knot in my stomach. It seemed strangely intimate—the idea of being alone in a dark room with the sheriff. *It's the library, not a motel*, I scolded myself.

"Do you know what you're doing?" the sheriff asked.

"No. I really don't," I said, my mind still on the knot.

In the darkness, I sensed him looking at me. "We're talking about the book, right?"

"Yes. Absolutely."

He scooted his chair closer. "And what is it that we're looking at anyway?"

"A rare book about rare toxins. I'm hoping to find something that matches the symptoms of the tepen's poison." I hesitated. "I guess we don't both need to read it."

"Two sets of eyes are always better than one. One of us might notice something the other one misses. If you're worried, I promise not to read over your shoulder. I know how much you hate that."

Ugh, I really did hate that. "How can we see it together if you don't read over my shoulder?"

"We can each take a turn reading a page," he suggested.

"The problem is that one of us has to sit in silence while the other one reads. You know I won't be very good at that."

"What do you suggest then?" He was close enough that his soft breath caressed the curve of my neck and I shivered in response. This suddenly seemed like a bad idea.

"How about we alternate reading and anything relevant, we read out loud so the other one hears?"

He scratched the stubble on his chiseled jaw. "Sure. Let's give it a try. Just promise not to mock me if I mispronounce anything."

"As long as you don't say 'supposably' or 'liberry,' we're good."

"Ladies first." He motioned to the tray where the book was already open to the index page. The book rested beneath a transparent dome of magical energy.

I leaned over and scanned the index for relevant terms. "Turn to page 71." The pages flipped until they reached the requested page. I skimmed the contents, searching for anything that might help us identify the mystery poison.

My pulse accelerated when I reached the middle paragraph. "Here's something. A drop of poison from the vasuki demon serpent causes a similar condition to that of the tepen's poison."

"By condition, you mean dropping dead?"

"Well, that's the final outcome, after the blue skin and lips. Despite the fact that they live on different continents, some experts believe they might be related."

"Sounds like a possibility."

"Except that monster is as rare as the tepen," I said, continuing to scan the page. "It's not like it would be an easy substitute for the killer." I raised my hand to turn the page, forgetting about the magical dome. My hand smacked into the invisible force and I shook off the stab of pain.

"That's a pretty bracelet," the sheriff said. "A gift from someone special?"

"Yes, from my aunt to me," I said with a laugh. "Not sure if she knows it yet though."

"I won't ask."

I paused to admire the emerald. "Raoul thinks it's going to fall off without me noticing and I'll lose it, but so far, so good."

"Jewelry looks good on you. You should wear more of it." He reached out and tucked strands of my hair behind my ear. "Maybe a nice pair of earrings to match."

I jumped to my feet in response to his touch, my heart hammering in my chest. "You know what? I have a million things to do today. Why don't you read up on these rare toxins and see if anything matches the effects of tepen poison and I'll grab the other books from Delphine on my way out?"

"Rose, I didn't mean…"

I started for the door, my palms sweating. "I'll let you know if I find anything." I stumbled out of the library, my head filled with competing thoughts, and tossed the books in my bag without a backward glance.

As I bolted from the library, I nearly barreled down a woman on the sidewalk, prompting a loud string of curses from her.

"Gods, I'm so sorry," I said.

She glanced from her phone to me. "Oh, I wasn't cursing at you. It's my game that's pissing me off." Her straight blond hair brushed her shoulders and she wore a black hoodie with rainbow sparkles, Star Wars sneakers, and leggings covered in sharks with a large set of jaws nestled in an inappropriate place. I glanced down and realized that three cats were sprawled at her feet. A woman traveling with a cat entourage?

"You're Amanda M'Leigh," I said.

She ignored me, concentrating on her phone.

"Is everything okay?" I asked.

"I should ask you the same thing. You look ready to throw up a hairball. I'll clean up theirs, but I won't clean up yours."

I regained my composure. "I'm fine, thanks."

The banshee waved her phone at me. "Do you know how hard it is to catch this shiny?"

"Shiny what?"

She narrowed her eyes. "I can already tell we're not going to get along."

"I'm Ember Rose." I thrust out my hand, but she ignored me and continued tapping on her screen.

"I can't do pleasantries. If I don't catch this sucker, I'm going to have a meltdown and, trust me, nobody wants that."

"Can't be worse than my aunt after she loses a game of parcheesi." The icy look she gave me suggested I was dead wrong.

"Parcheesi sounds like a type of pasta."

"Go ahead and catch your sparkly. I'll wait." I perched on the nearby stone wall and watched her finger circle round and round on the screen.

"Yes!" She pumped her fist in the air and tucked away her phone. "Mission accomplished. Now I can focus."

"Is that Wizards Connect?"

Amanda grimaced. "Do I look like an amateur to you? Now how can I help you, Ember Rose? Is that your stripper name or your real name?"

"Hey!" I slid off the stone wall. "I'm a reporter for *Vox Populi* and I need to ask you a few questions about your reasons for visiting Starry Hollow."

She groaned. "This is not how I want to spend my break time. I need a latte. Where's the nearest coffee shop?"

"The Caffeinated Cauldron isn't far. Can your latte wait five minutes?"

"Fine," she huffed, "but I'm going to play while we walk so I can hatch an egg."

I frowned. "A tepen egg?"

Her glance would've withered a live oak behind the cottage. "I don't have time for stupid questions."

I squared my shoulders and put on my best reporter face. "I understand you're here to obtain ingredients for your cosmetics company. You Glow Girl is a great name, by the way."

"I know. Have you seen our ads?" She waved her free hand in a dramatic fashion. "When pixie dust and blush collide."

"I don't know that I want anything colliding on my face."

She inspected my face. "Yeah, I can see that. A little dark spot corrector wouldn't kill you. We have an excellent product for that. You can order it from any of the major retailers."

"I just wear big sunglasses."

"That might work for dark circles under your eye, but it won't distract anyone from those age spots on your cheek."

I clenched my fists in an effort not to throat punch her. "I know that you're interested in procuring some kind of secretion from the tepen and I don't even like saying the word."

"Tepen?" she queried.

"No, secretion." I shuddered.

Amanda cackled. "Made you say it again."

I glared at her. "How exactly do you intend to do it?"

"Sorry. I don't reveal company trade secrets, certainly not to the press."

"How is that a trade secret?"

"It's a secret related to my trade, ergo, trade secret." A strange sound emanated from her phone.

"Did your phone just go *pew pew pew*?"

She ignored me as she tapped her screen to check the notification. "There's another one."

"Another sparkler?"

She tapped on her screen. "You're mine."

"If you're this aggressive about catching the tepen, I'm surprised you haven't managed it yet."

"I would have if the whole Winston York thing hadn't happened."

"You think his death is the reason you haven't found the tepen? I would think the fact that you're here playing a game on your phone might be a factor."

She cackled again. "You obviously don't know the first thing about me if you think this game will somehow interfere with me getting my work done."

"Do your cats always follow you around like some kind of feline Pied Piper?"

She spared a glance at them. "They're spoiled rotten. They travel everywhere with me. That's Arwen, Bilbo, and Bay." She pointed from left to right.

I stared at the calico cats. "Why do you travel with them?"

"I have to. They don't like anyone except me. I've tried sitters, but the cats either scare everyone off or send them to the healer for stitches."

"I can see why that's a problem." Looking at them now as they purred contentedly on the pavement, it was hard to imagine that they were the ferocious beasts that Amanda claimed.

"At least I have my own plane. Makes it much easier to travel with three cats, plus I get to avoid security. The last time I had to fly commercial, I spent an hour getting a full-body pat down. By the time she finished, I felt like I should pay her."

"That reminds me. I had dinner with your pal Lionel Lattimer last night."

"Sorry to hear that. How did you end up in that unfortunate situation?"

"He's friends with my aunt."

"She must be a real charmer."

I laughed. "You have no idea. So, have you had many run-ins with Winston York over the years?"

"No, as a matter of fact, this trip is the first time I've ever met him."

"But you knew who he was before this?"

"Of course." She stepped over Arwen and held up her phone. "Got you!" She tapped on her screen with a triumphant finger before returning her focus to me. "Everyone knows who Winston York is. I spent my childhood watching his programs. Actually, it's where I got one of my first ideas for a product. It was the one where he featured a gormo. They're extinct now, but their excess milk was known for its moisturizing properties."

"Did you meet him while you searched for the tepen?"

"No, the only bozos I saw were Lattimer, that tree hugger Heidelberg, and the Winston wannabe."

"There's a Winston wannabe?"

Pew pew pew.

She glanced at her phone. "I already have that one." She tossed her phone into her handbag adorned with Kim Kardashian's face. Amanda was a big fan of the human world, it seemed. "I don't remember his name. He wants to be the next York. Used to work for him."

My pulse sped up. This could be helpful information. "And you saw him in Starry Hollow?"

"Yeah, we were both in the woods searching for the nest. He thought he found tracks, but they belonged to a raccoon."

I snorted as I made a mental note to find out the mystery guy's name. "Are you like Lionel Lattimer? You fly around when there's a report of a rare creature and try to capture it for your lab?"

The look she gave me would've frozen water. "I am nothing like that loser Lattimer."

"And what about Winston? When did you meet him?"

"I met him on the beach and then we met up for drinks later in the evening."

"For drinks? Where did you meet him?"

"The old place by the water." She snapped her fingers in

an effort to jog her memory. "The place with the weird vampire pirate behind the bar."

"The Whitethorn."

"That's the one. Cool place. Reminds me of a hobbit house."

"Bilbo and Arwen must've taken a shine to it."

She smiled at the cats. "The parrot wasn't too excited about my entourage. He flew off in a huff and the pirate said he probably wouldn't come back until the cats were gone."

"You spared yourself a few insults in that case."

"Yeah, I hate parrots. They look like feathered clowns."

I wanted to know more about this meeting of the minds. "What did you talk about?"

"Our travels. He asked me if I had any insight on the tepen."

"Do you?"

She shrugged. "No more than he did. He asked me to pack up and go home, of course, but I expected that."

"I guess you refused."

Amanda cursed again as her phone lit up. "I treat my captives with respect, not like that butcher Lattimer."

"And that was the only time you saw York—at the Whitethorn?"

"That's it. Incredible guy. I'm sorry he's dead, even if we didn't see eye-to-eye."

I'd have to check out her story while she was still on the hunt for the tepen. "Where are you staying while you're in town?"

"Well, I was staying at the Lighthouse Inn, but I changed to the Pegasus Palace because apparently topless swimming is frowned upon there." She rolled her eyes.

"I'm surprised you have time for swimming and gaming."

She lifted her chin a fraction. "I'm an organizational ninja."

I was tempted to ask if she was offering lessons, but I already had more than my fair share of those. "Good luck on your quest."

"Thanks." Her nose was already back in front of the screen and I heard another string of expletives as I rounded the corner. It occurred to me that if I ever decided to try gaming as a leisure activity, the only part I'd be any good at was the cursing.

CHAPTER THIRTEEN

"ARE you sure you don't mind if I meet Alec at the Whitethorn later?" I asked. "I can call Mrs. Babcock if it would make you feel better."

Marley glanced up from her place on the couch where her nose was buried in a book. "My head is so full of spells I have to memorize that I won't have any room for anxiety."

"The upside of a heavy workload," I said. My phone lit up and Artemis's name flashed on the screen. "Uh oh. This doesn't bode well."

"Artemis?" Marley queried.

I scanned the message. "She wants me to come over. There's an issue with Ackley and Aspen."

Marley continued reviewing her book. "It's okay, Mom. Like I said, I'll just be doing schoolwork. Do whatever you need to do."

Raoul, will you hang out with her tonight? I know she said she's fine, but still.

Are you kidding? I want to see what's happening over there. I bet the twins are swinging from the chandelier and Jefferson can't get them down.

I crossed my arms and glared at him. *Artemis doesn't need an audience.*

Fine, then I'll go as your accountability coach. Bonkers is here. She can look after Marley. He motioned to the flying kitten currently digging her claws into the scratching post.

"You two don't need to argue in your heads," Marley interjected. "I don't mind."

I turned to smile at her. "There's no need for us to distract you from schoolwork."

"Just go, Mom. Make sure Artemis is okay. Spend time with Alec. I can handle being on my own." She inclined her head toward the couch where PP3 was snoring. "Besides, I have a chaperone."

Tears pricked my eyes. My little girl was growing up right before my eyes. I still remembered when she would cry and cling to my leg at kindergarten drop-off. How was this composed young witch the same person?

I grabbed my handbag from the end table. "Call me if you need anything and definitely call me to say goodnight."

Raoul shadowed me as I left the cottage, probably afraid that I'd make a run for it. *I call shotgun.*

"You don't have to call shotgun when you're the only passenger."

He fixed his dark eyes on me. *Then how about I drive?*

"Are you insane?" I unlocked the car and slid behind the wheel.

Raoul climbed into the passenger seat. *Is it such a crazy idea? If that puny leprechaun can reach the pedals, so can I.*

"It's not about reaching the pedals. It's about actually driving. You're a raccoon." I pulled the car away from the house and set off down the driveway.

He rested his paws behind his head. *I don't think you're thinking this through. If I drive, that enables you to do all sorts of things.*

I squinted at him. "Like what?"

I can run errands for you. Pick up your dry cleaning.

"I never have dry cleaning. If a tag says dry clean only, it goes back on the rack."

He tapped his paw against his face, thinking. *I can go through the drive-thru for you so you don't have to leave the house.*

My hands froze on the wheel. "Now that's a worthwhile skill."

I could even do the taco truck.

I mulled it over. "How much trouble might we be in if Bolan catches you behind the wheel?"

Nothing you can't get out of. Tell him I took the car without your permission. He'll believe that.

Yes, he definitely would. Raoul's shady past oftentimes caught up with him. "Let me think about it."

That's adult speak for no.

"How about there's no speak for five minutes? I'm having trouble hearing myself think with you constantly talking."

But I'm bringing life to the voice inside your head.

I gave him a pointed look. "You *are* the voice inside my head. That's the problem."

That's my job right now, remember? My goal is to push you to do better. To up your stagnant game. Isn't that what you want?

I wrinkled my nose. "You shouldn't use words like stagnant."

He looked aggrieved. *Why not? I'm clever enough.*

"I know, but it conjures images of flies circling piles of trash."

He settled against the back of the seat. *Now I'm hungry.*

I pulled in front of Haverford House and parked the car. "You're supposed to be providing assistance in a nonjudgmental way. That's what accountability coaches do. Otherwise, you're just a surrogate mother." Or, in my case, aunt.

How am I judgmental? Do I comment when you go to bed

without flossing your teeth? Do I open my mouth when you add cinnamon to what would otherwise be excellent oatmeal? No. No, I do not. His huff was full of aggravation.

"Let's table this for later. I have to rescue poor Artemis from these blond balls of energy."

I hurried to the door and waited for Jefferson to answer. A few minutes later, the door creaked open and Artemis stood there in her white lace dress and a troubled expression.

"Oh, thank the goddess."

I stepped inside with Raoul right behind me. "Where's Jefferson?"

"He's trying to entice the boys to come down from the roof."

My heart began to pound. "The roof?"

"Yes, they wanted to take turns on my broomstick," Artemis said. "They were very insistent and I wasn't quick enough to stop them."

"They can't see or hear Jefferson. How can a ghost entice them to do anything?"

Artemis pursed her lips. "I don't know exactly. Jefferson said he would handle it so I let him."

Raoul licked his paw and smoothed down the wayward fur on his head. *I'll take care of it. You stay here with Artemis.*

I glanced quizzically at my raccoon familiar. "Are you sure?"

I have a feeling if you get up there, it'll only escalate.

"Okay." I smiled at Artemis. "Raoul is going to give Jefferson a hand…paw on the roof."

"Wonderful. Thank you so much." She seemed to notice my outfit for the first time. "You look very dressed up for an evening at home."

I glanced down at my dress. "Oh, that's because I'm meeting Alec out for a drink."

"Date night, is it?" she asked slyly.

"Sort of. I need to follow up on something at the Whitethorn for an article I'm writing and we figured we'd combine the two."

"Sounds lovely. Would you like a cup of tea while you wait?"

"Sure." I knew how much Artemis enjoyed the role of hostess and I wasn't about to deprive her of it. My aunt, on the other hand, was another story.

I sat on the settee in the parlor room and checked in with Marley while I waited for the elderly witch to return with my tea. A few minutes later, Artemis meandered into the room with a cup and saucer shaking in her unsteady hand. Every nerve in my body was screaming to rush in and rescue the cup before she spilled it, but I resisted the urge to swoop in and insult her. The elderly witch finally reached the loveseat and, as she leaned back to sit, I swiped the cup and saucer and set them carefully on the coffee table.

"I'm glad we were able to help you out," I said. "I would've felt terrible if they'd burned down your house or something." I laughed awkwardly.

"Oh, they're not that naughty. I just worry about them so high up. I know Aster hasn't introduced them to very much in the way of magic."

"No, not yet. I'm surprised they're not afraid of Jefferson," I said. "It's not as though any of us have our own ghost."

"I think it's because they can't see him, so they feel they don't have to answer to him."

I slurped my tea. "Actually, even if they could see him, they wouldn't feel they had to answer to him. They're at that stage where they're testing boundaries as well as patience."

Raoul returned to the parlor room looking satisfied.

I rose to my feet, my throat thickening at the sight of the raccoon by himself. "What happened? Where are the boys?"

In bed. They let Jefferson tuck them in.

"How did you manage that feat?"

I pretended to have rabies and foamed at the mouth until they ran to Jefferson to save them. He scooped them up and carried them off.

"Ah, fear is an excellent motivator," I said.

I'll remember that the next time you complain about your aunt.

I calmed Artemis with a relaxed smile. "The boys are in bed now. Jefferson tucked them in safely."

"Thank the goddess for that." Artemis clucked her tongue. "I forget how naughty little wizards can be. It's been quite some time since I had dealings with any."

"I'm sorry they were so much trouble."

"It's quite all right, Ember. I thought I could keep them in line with magic, but I don't use spells the way I used to. I couldn't even find my wand." Her pale eyes sparked with a memory. "Speaking of wands, how is Marley making out with the one she inherited from that ancestor of yours?"

"Hmm." I wasn't sure how much I wanted to divulge—not that I didn't trust Artemis, but she was the town matchmaker and had more foot traffic than the Starry Hollow podiatrist. Telling her that I accessed Ivy's magic would increase the risk of Hyacinth finding out.

Artemis seemed to sense my apprehension. "I'm sorry, dear. I shouldn't have asked. It's none of my concern."

"It isn't that…" It would be nice to have a witch to confide in—someone who understood the history. "There are things about the situation that bother me."

"I see."

Tell her, Raoul urged from beside me on the settee.

I don't know that I should.

She's ancient. She won't remember tomorrow. Get her advice and get out.

I rolled my eyes. *This is your advice as my accountability coach?*

No, I'm wearing my familiar hat now.

Is it made of raccoon fur? Because that hasn't been in vogue since Davy Crockett.

"Would you like anything else?" Artemis offered. "Another drink or a biscuit?"

"No, thank you. We're good."

Don't speak for me. He raised a paw. *I'll have a pepperoni pizza with a burrito on the side.*

I slapped a throw pillow over his face. "Are you really interested in hearing more about Ivy?"

"Yes, absolutely." Artemis leaned forward and lifted her cup to her cracked lips. Either she was in desperate need of Chapstick or Jefferson wasn't giving her much time to come up for air, although I wasn't quite sure how hanky panky worked with a ghost—nor did I want to.

"I have Ivy's Book of Shadows and I seem to have accessed the magic she'd hidden away before they stripped her of the rest of it."

Artemis barely reacted. "And you're worried about Hyacinth?"

"I don't know if worried is the right word. I'm suspicious."

"You think she wants that power."

I nodded, wanting to unburden myself. "I think the whole reason she gave Marley those gifts is because she believed that Marley would be able to unlock the magic somehow and that, once Hyacinth finds out, she'll swoop in and try to take it for herself."

"And you feel conflicted because you want to trust your aunt."

My eyes grew moist. Artemis was right. I did want to trust her, but I knew I couldn't. "Honestly, everyone close to me lies. I should be used to it by now."

Her smile was sympathetic. "Like your father."

"I don't blame him for what he did. I know he was only trying to protect me." From the very aunt I didn't trust—the one who seemed hungry for power and willing to go the distance to get it.

"Still, it would be understandable if you were angry with your father. He hid an entire part of your life from you. A part of yourself."

"How can I be angry with him? He's dead. There's no point. I can't yell at him. I can't ask questions." I slumped against the cushion. How did we get here? I'd only intended to help her with the twins and now I was in a therapy session.

"Don't resist those feelings, however uncomfortable, Ember."

I swallowed the remainder of my tea. "I would appreciate keeping this between us. I don't want anyone to know about Ivy's magic. She has such a bad reputation."

"But you're not Ivy, dear. Remember that. Her magic... Her power. You're still you, no matter what you have access to."

"I threw Wren across a clearing like he was a ball," I admitted.

She laughed lightly. "He probably enjoyed that."

I smiled. "He did."

She reached forward and patted my knee. "Try not to worry. The answer will come to you when the time is right. In the meantime, you handle it however you deem best."

"It's a lot of power," I said. "I become more aware of it when I'm about to fall asleep. I've had nightmares."

"Because your defenses are down. You're probably resisting it during your waking hours."

"Why would I do that?"

"Because you're afraid, of course."

I nodded. "I think I am." Afraid and yet also relieved that

it was me and not Marley carrying this burden. She was far too young and inexperienced. At least I was old and inexperienced.

The doorbell rang, startling both of us.

"That must be Aster and Sterling," Artemis said. "Jefferson will answer it."

"Not a word to Aster, okay?"

Artemis met my pleading gaze and nodded, almost imperceptibly.

My cousin came rushing into the parlor room. She looked beautiful with her hair in a chignon and wearing a hot pink dress. Her brow furrowed when she saw me.

"I thought that was your car. Is everything okay? The boys weren't too much trouble, were they?"

"Not at all," Artemis said. "They were little angels. Where's Sterling?"

"Waiting in the car."

"The boys are asleep upstairs. I can have Jefferson carry them down if you'd prefer not to wake them."

"That would be wonderful, thank you." Aster fixed her gaze on me. "You left Marley alone at this hour?"

I shrugged. "She said she'd be fine. My little girl isn't so little anymore."

"And how was your evening out?" Artemis asked.

My eyes widened. "Yes. How *was* your evening? Any progress on the thing we talked about?"

Aster smiled. "We'll discuss it later." Two white-blond wizards floated into the room, their eyes closed and mouths open. "There are my sweet boys." She glanced back at Artemis. "Thank you so much. You're a lifesaver."

"It was lovely to have such youthful energy in the house again. It's been far too long."

One of the things I loved about Artemis was her sweet disposition. If she told you your boys were angels straight sent from Heaven, whether she truly believed that or not, you knew she wasn't going to turn around and bad mouth them to someone else.

"I hate to run, but I need to meet Alec," I said.

"Make the most of your time together," Artemis said.

Raoul gave me a hopeful look as we left the house. *Can we stop at a drive-thru on the way home? I'm hungry.*

I looked at him agape. *You had a whole tin of biscuits. Don't deny it. I heard you in the kitchen before you came back to the parlor room.*

And now I need salty to counteract the sweet.

"I've got salty for you right here," I said in a threatening tone.

Forget it, he mumbled. *I don't like when you speak mobster. I'll make my own way home.*

"Works for me. I'm driving straight to the Whitethorn anyway and you're not invited."

Don't forget to hold yourself accountable.

I frowned as I opened the car door. "You mean don't drink and drive?"

He rolled his eyes. *Obviously not, but I'm talking about Alec.*

"What about him?" I slid behind the wheel and started the car.

Raoul stood next to the driver's side door. *You want to establish realistic goals that help you move forward in all areas of your life. That includes Mr. Tall, Toned, and Fanged. He's either part of the solution or he's part of the problem.*

I'm not having this conversation with you. I started to back out of the driveway, careful not to run over his paws.

Then you need to have it with him. It's time, Ember. You've let him off the hook long enough.

What hook? There's no hook. In the darkness, I saw the raccoon's eyes shine.

One that would have the fruit must first climb the tree.

If I wanted a fortune, I'd have ordered Chinese food, I said.

Be not afraid of growing slowly, be afraid only of standing still.

"I am not doing this with you right now!" I pulled alongside him and rolled down the window. "If you want the rainbow, you have to tolerate the rain!"

Raoul trained his small, dark eyes on me. *It's been raining long enough and I don't see any rainbows, do you?*

I rolled up the window and sped off in anger, watching in the rearview mirror as the darkness swallowed him.

CHAPTER FOURTEEN

I ARRIVED AT THE WHITETHORN, determined to forget my argument with Raoul and enjoy the rest of my evening without his fortune cookie proverbs invading my headspace. His days as my accountability coach were unsurprisingly numbered. I'd been insane to accept his offer in the first place—or so mentally and emotionally overwhelmed that I was willing to accept any lifeline thrown my way.

I hovered outside the entrance and checked in with Marley to say good night before making my way into the pub. I was relieved that she sounded completely fine. She was in bed with PP3 and Bonkers and no one was growling or hissing. Success.

"Good evening, Captain Yellowjacket," I said, approaching the bar with a big smile.

"As I live and don't breathe," the vampire pirate said. He wore his trademark bright yellow jacket, black pirate hat, and, of course, an eye patch. As the descendant of the notorious Captain Blackfang, a vampire pirate that terrorized the high seas, he liked to dress the part. "If it isn't intrepid reporter Ember Rose. What brings you here this evening, lass

—business or pleasure?" His brow lifted as he glanced over my shoulder. "Aye. Pleasure it is then."

"Both, actually," I said.

His presumption made sense when Alec appeared beside me. He bent down to kiss my cheek. "You're a sight for sore eyes."

"Your eyes are sore because they've been locked on a screen all day. How's the book?"

"Coming along." He greeted Captain Yellowjacket with a firm handshake and ordered an ale. "Ember?"

"I'm still deciding." The tea from Haverford House had made me a little nauseous. Jefferson had a tendency to overdo the milk.

Captain Yellowjacket slid the glass across the bar to Alec. "Anything for you, lassie?"

"As a matter of fact, I need to ask you about a visitor you had here the other night. A blond banshee named Amanda M'Leigh. She would've been on her phone most of the time. It makes a *pew pew pew* sound."

Alec chuckled. "I didn't catch that. Can you make that sound again?"

I nudged him with my elbow.

"Aye, I saw the lass you mentioned. She was here with three cats and Winston York, the gods rest his merry soul." He lowered his head in a show of respect.

"Three cats?" Alec queried.

"They're spoiled and she takes them everywhere." I shifted my focus to Duncan. "Do you happen to remember what they ordered?"

He drummed his fingers on the counter. "She ordered for both of them. Two brambles."

"That's rum and burstberry ale in a cocktail?" I'd sampled it once before but didn't care for the ale.

"Aye. She finished hers first, but he nursed his for the duration of their chat."

"Would you say he drank any of it?" I asked.

He peered at me with his one good eye. "Why do you ask?"

"Just curious," I said.

"He might've sipped it to be polite, but when the glasses were brought back to the bar, his was full even taking into account the melted ice."

So if Amanda had poisoned him, it would have to be a toxin so strong that one anemic sip could do the deed, albeit many hours later. It seemed highly unlikely.

"Did you notice any strange odors or unusual residue from the glass?"

He recoiled. "Yar! I only use the best ingredients."

"Oh, I know. I'm sorry, Duncan. I'm not casting aspersions on your business practices, I swear."

"You don't think she was testing any of her products on Winston York, do you?" Captain Yellowjacket tugged his ear thoughtfully. "Now that you mention it, his skin looked much shinier by the time he left."

"Squawk!" Bittersteel flew over my head, his colorful feathers skimming the top of it, and slammed beak-first into the captain's shoulder. "Tell her!"

Captain Yellowjacket narrowed his eyes at the parrot, now perched on his shoulder swaying back and forth. "Do I need to get out the drunk tank for you again?"

"Liar!" The parrot punctuated his remark with a loud belch.

"You might want to slow down on the fermented grapes," I said.

Bittersteel refused to be silenced. "Tell her the truth!" The parrot shook his feathered head so hard that he tipped over.

He propelled his wings to keep himself from plunging to the floor.

I peered at the vampire pirate. "The truth? What's he talking about?"

The red of his already ruddy cheeks deepened from embarrassment. "Don't get the wrong idea, lassie. He only means that I might have finished the drink."

I stared at him blankly. "The drink?"

"Winston's drink. I despise the waste of alcohol…"

"Waste not, want not," the parrot squawked. He attempted to fly forward and ended up head-butting Alec.

"It seems to me you want for very little alcohol this evening." The stoic vampire gripped the parrot by the wing and flung him across the pub like a Frisbee.

"Sometimes if a customer seems to have left a drink untouched, I'll finish it." Captain Yellowjacket exhaled loudly. "There, I said it." He glanced around furtively. "Please don't tell anyone. I don't need health and safety officers swarming the place."

His confession ruled out a poison drink from Amanda. I leaned across the counter to pat his cheek. "Actually, your honesty has been a huge help. Thank you."

Captain Yellowjacket squared his shoulders and grinned, flashing a gold fang. "I figured it was Winston York. Living legend. How bad could his germs be?"

"You're a vampire, Duncan," Alec said. "The chances of you being felled by any germs you might pick up in a shared drink are infinitesimal."

"Too true, me hearty. The worst I suffer is the occasional bout of indigestion that follows too many Yorkshire puddings."

Alec covered his hand with mine. "Shall we retreat to a booth or do you have more questions?"

"No, I'm good." At least I could rule out Amanda. *Take that, Raoul. Another box ticked.*

"I'll send over a couple of menus," Captain Yellowjacket said.

I waved him off. "No need. Unless you've changed it, I think I know it by heart."

Alec and I settled across from each other in a dimly lit booth. "Have I mentioned how lovely you look this evening?"

"No. I'm all ears." I cupped a hand to my ear, prompting a light laugh from the vampire.

"You look lovely this evening, Ember."

His voice alone made me shiver with delight. He could read mortgage documents to me and I'd still want to jump his bones. Raoul's words floated through my mind. *You want to establish realistic goals that help you move forward in all areas of your life. That includes Mr. Tall, Toned, and Fanged. He's either part of the solution or he's part of the problem.*

"Is everything all right?" Alec asked. "You seem preoccupied."

I shoved the thoughts aside and forced a smile. "Everything is great."

We skipped the appetizers and ordered two main courses and a bottle of wine. Once the wine had been poured, Alec focused those mesmerizing eyes on me.

"If I didn't know any better, I'd say you were investigating Amanda M'Leigh for some reason. Did you unearth anything newsworthy about her? Aside from the charming sound her phone makes, of course."

I swallowed hard. I didn't want to lie to Alec, but I'd promised the sheriff that I'd keep York's murder to myself. I had to honor that promise. It was basically the same as protecting a source from my editor. Good thing I'd mastered the art of cloaking my thoughts from the vampire.

"Sort of. I spoke to her as part of my research on York

and I think she'd make a good story for the paper, after I'm finished writing about Winston, of course."

If he sensed there was more to it than that, he didn't push the issue. "Speaking of a good story, you just gave me an idea for the chapter I'm working on." He pulled out his phone and began typing a note to himself.

I decided to send the sheriff a quick update on Amanda while Alec was distracted. Our meals arrived just as I hit send.

"Checking on Marley?" he asked.

"Yes," I lied and immediately felt a surge of guilt. "She's still awake."

"We can eat quickly if you're in a rush to get home."

"No, she's fine, but I appreciate the offer." I desperately wanted to enjoy my quality time with Alec. It felt like forever since we'd sat across from each other, alone and without a computer between us.

The food was delicious and, for the next half an hour, there was nothing in the world except the two of us. Alec was his magnetic self and we couldn't resist touching each other during the meal, even though it was only our shoes meeting under the table. The topics I'd intended to discuss fell by the wayside and I just enjoyed being present in the moment with him.

By the time we left the pub, Bittersteel was on a table by the door beak-deep in a pint of ale with his eyes closed. I was pretty sure I heard him snoring.

"I hope Duncan has a hangover cure for that parrot," I said, laughing as we stood under a blanket of twinkling stars.

Alec took my hand. "Care for a stroll on the beach before we go our separate ways?"

"Best Journey song there is."

His brow knitted together. "Journey?"

"Rock band. I'd sing it for you, but I can't hit the high

notes like my man Steve Perry. A stroll sounds romantic. Let's do it."

"You're certain? I understand if you'd rather go home."

I slipped off my shoes and held them in my hand. "Not me. I'm all for grabbing life by the unicorn horn."

His mouth twitched. "You have the most charming expressions."

I looked at him, experimenting with a variety of faces. "I do, don't I? I'm a big fan of this one." I showed him the 'extreme smile,' which was the hideous face I made in New Jersey when I received unwanted attention from men. It was a cross between The Joker and Marie Osmond—all crazy eyes and teeth.

"Very attractive, indeed."

The moonlight rippled across the water and I released a happy sigh. "Before I forget, I wasn't able to get the appointment with that new therapist. She was booked for the next two months, so I need to keep looking."

He squeezed my hand. "I think we have enough to occupy us these days, wouldn't you agree?"

"You can take a break from your book. You know I'm always willing to make time for us."

His thumb gently stroked my hand. "It's always something though, isn't it? If not the book, then other duties crop up that require immediate attention. The list is Sisyphean."

"That's life, I guess, which brings me back to my original point of grabbing life by the unicorn horn. For all York's flaws, he lived a good, full life."

"I envy him that."

I cast a sidelong glance at him. "You're a vampire with an impressive career. Why would you envy his life?"

"Because it gets to be complete. Winston York enjoyed a beginning, a middle, and an end. I'll never experience that."

I listened to the waves as they crashed against the shore.

Normally I found the sound soothing, but right now I was too unnerved to appreciate it.

I stopped walking and let my feet sink into the sand. "Alec, are you having some sort of immortal life crisis?"

His attempt at light laughter didn't fool me. "Is that how it sounds?"

I decided to take Raoul's advice and try to nudge us forward. "Yes. You've been immersing yourself in this new series and spending less time with me. You're distracted. You're more critical than usual." I hadn't intended to unleash my feelings, especially during a romantic walk on the beach, but the opportunity seemed ripe.

His broad shoulders stiffened. "Everything is fine. I'm sorry you feel differently."

"It's okay to be in a rut, or whatever it is. I just wish you would feel that you can talk to me about it."

"As I said, everything is fine. I've been spending time in this new book because I find joy there."

"And you're not able to find joy here, in the real world with me?" A breeze whipped through my hair, blowing strands into my mouth. My hair was like a hydra. Every time I pulled one piece out of my mouth, two more strands blew in.

"That's not what I meant. Can we not do this, please?" He started walking back toward the Whitethorn and I hurried after him.

"If protecting yourself continues to be your main priority, then I don't see how we can ever have a fully functioning relationship."

Alec halted and gazed at me with the kind of intensity that made my body burn and my mind go blank.

"You're right, Ember," he said, his voice barely audible over the crashing of the waves. "I need to do better or I don't deserve to be in a relationship with you."

Hope bloomed in my chest. "Then you'll try therapy again? I'll make sure to find someone…"

He didn't let me finish. "No, I've decided that's not the right avenue for me. If I have trouble sharing myself with you, I don't see how including a stranger in the mix will help matters."

"I'm not talking about some rando off the street."

He shook his head. "I'm sorry, Ember."

Petals of hope shriveled and I hugged myself to keep from crying. "Then what do we do?"

"There are plenty of books on the topic. I can choose the most relevant ones and simply implement their suggestions."

"You'll just get lost in another book," I said. "That's not called communicating. That's called reading."

Why had I listened to Raoul? Now we were arguing and the evening was ruined. This wasn't what I wanted.

Alec brushed the hair from my cheek. "I know you're feeling overwhelmed right now. I see no reason to add to your list of concerns."

"You and Marley *are* my main concerns." I fought the urge to argue further. "If you want to dive into relationship research, then I'll support you."

He tipped my chin up and brushed his lips against mine. "You needn't worry, Ember. Whatever challenges we face, our love will sustain us."

I melted into the kiss and ignored the faint voice in my head, not Raoul's this time, but my own. The voice that dared to ask the question I'd been unwilling to entertain—what if love wasn't enough?

CHAPTER FIFTEEN

THE NEXT MORNING, I sailed into the office of *Vox Populi* wearing oversized sunglasses and a baseball hat.

Bentley glanced up with a quizzical expression. "Being stalked by paparazzi again, Britney?"

I walked over to my desk and set down my bag. "I had a late night."

"Apparently."

I removed the sunglasses. "I woke up feeling a little longer in the tooth than usual."

"What does that mean?"

"Old, Bentley." I whipped off the hat. "It means old."

"Since when do you care about that?"

I looked at him askance. "Since when don't I care about that? I have an ego, you know."

"Right, and I thought that ego told you that you look amazing even in a potato sack and bright orange lipstick."

"You seem to have me confused with Hazel." I settled in my chair beside him. "I think it's these cosmetics company owners. Amanda made me feel like I need a face transplant and, this morning, I spotted two gray hairs at my scalp. If I leave them alone together too long, they'll make babies."

"You're worried about a couple of gray hairs?" Bentley scoffed. "That doesn't sound like something to waste your energy on."

My gaze darted to the private office at the back of the room. "That's because Meadow isn't a vampire."

Bentley seemed to grasp my meaning. "You're worried that your aging will bother your immortal boyfriend?"

"It's hard to know what he's thinking half the time because he doesn't talk about it, which leaves me to fill in the blanks on my own." I booted up my computer and swiveled toward him. "I'm very good at filling in blanks with what's in my head, Bentley."

"Sounds dangerous." He offered a sympathetic look. "I wouldn't worry, Ember. I've seen the way he looks at you and, trust me, I wish I didn't. It's the same way a lion looks at a gazelle."

I cocked my head. "Alec looks at me like he wants to hide in the tall grass of a savannah and pounce when I go to my watering hole?"

"Something like that," he mumbled.

I noticed the Nash folder open on his desk. "How's your research coming along? Any progress on the cold case?"

Bentley held the folder protectively against his chest. "Why? Is your article done and you've come to claim mine?"

"Relax. I'm not here to poach. In fact, I'm glad you're taking an interest in it."

His brow lifted. "Really?"

"Yeah. You're good at your job. What if you find something that gives the Nash family closure?" I wanted that for Granger and his mom—and even for Wyatt, that swaggering hormone.

Relief flooded Bentley's expression. "I'm glad to hear you say that because I may have made progress."

I nearly leaped across the desk divider to wrench the folder from his hands. "What did you find?"

He rolled his chair further away from me, creating a foot-long gap. "I'd rather not say yet. I just thought you'd be interested to know that I think there's a real story here."

I smiled sweetly. "Come on, Bentley, old pal. Don't keep a friend in suspense. Tell me what you learned."

"Why? So you can get drunk and confess it all to the sheriff? I don't think so." He shoved the folder partway down the front of his pants.

"Clever choice. You know I have no interest in grabbing you there."

Bentley held out a hand to keep me at bay. "I promise I'll tell you when I find something worth sharing. Right now, it's just a step forward based on something small that I found."

I relaxed in my chair and turned back to my computer. "Fine. I won't pester you…about that."

The front door opened and a figure peered inside. His shaggy brown hair was shoulder-length and he wore a sleeveless black shirt which showed off an owl tattoo. There was something vaguely familiar about him.

"Hey, is this *Vox Populi*?"

"Who wants to know?" I demanded.

"Ember," Bentley hissed under his breath. "That's no way to greet a potential source."

"Source for what?" I whispered. "Which hair salons to avoid?"

"Sorry to interrupt. I'm looking for Ember Rose." He tucked his hair behind his ear, revealing a pointy tip. Never in a million years would I have pegged him for an elf.

"Oh, that's me."

He seemed relieved. "Awesome. Glad I found you. I'm Bruce Magill."

I stood to shake his hand. "Nice to meet you. How can I help you?"

"I'm a filmmaker. In fact, I was Winston York's protege for years."

And then it hit me. I'd seen him with York in a photo on the wall of the workshop. "I'm so sorry for your loss."

He pressed his lips together. "Yeah, thanks. I always thought the old curmudgeon was going to live forever, you know. Such a pillar of our global community."

His words failed to register. I was too busy staring at his owl tattoo as the head twisted 180 degrees. Bentley must've noticed too because I heard his gasp of delight behind me.

Bruce glanced at his bicep. "Cool, right? I had it done at this place called Spelling Ink. The witch there creates all sorts of awesome magical tattoos."

"Is that here in town?" Bentley asked. "I haven't heard of it."

"No, I was making a short film in Spellbound. It's this Pennsylvania town that had been under a curse…"

My eyes popped. "I've been there. Alec…My editor and I went after the curse was broken to write a story about it."

His head bobbed with enthusiasm. "Pretty awesome place, right?"

"I don't think that tattoo parlor was there yet." I watched the owl in wonder as it opened and closed its beak. "It doesn't hoot?"

"Begonia gave me the option of sound, but I chose a muted one," Bruce said. "In my line of work, I often need silence or I scare off the subjects."

"Right. Your work." His identity finally registered. "You're the successor who was searching for the nest in the woods. You ran into Amanda M'Leigh."

"The cosmetics owner, right?" He fluffed his hair again. It seemed to me that his hair would be more of a distraction during filming than a hooting owl tattoo.

"Yes. There are two of them in town trying to get to the tepen first," I said.

Bruce scowled. "Big business is the worst. They destroy our environment. Kill our creatures. All for a tidy profit."

A vague smile touched my lips. "You sound like Jarek Heidelberg."

"Well, except he goes one step further and thinks *we* interfere with the natural world," Bruce said. "He lumps me into the same category as cosmetics and trophy hunters and that's minotaur shit. I revere the creatures I track. I would never do anything to hurt them."

I leaned back in my chair. "What brings you here?"

"I understand you took possession of Winston's recording. The raw footage he'd shot before he died."

"Sorry, I'm no longer in possession of that."

He frowned. "Can you tell me where it is now? I want to be able to pick up where he left off."

"The sheriff has it."

Bruce scratched behind his ear. "Why would law enforcement want it?"

"Just a formality," I lied. "He died on Starry Hollow property so the sheriff holds on to any personal effects at the scene until the estate's been settled."

"That should be easy enough. It was only he and his wife. They didn't have any kids or close relations."

"I didn't get the impression that Mabel would be interested in keeping it," I said.

"No, you're right. She'll probably let me have it. The only reason she might hesitate to release it is because it includes his final moments, at least that's what I heard."

"I can't imagine she'd want to watch that on a loop." Bentley shuddered.

"I certainly wouldn't include that in my film," Bruce said. "I'm not a monster. I'd just like the rest of it. Any footage of the tepen is extremely valuable, however limited."

"As I said, you'll have to take that up with the sheriff. It's literally out of my hands." Why else would he want the footage other than to erase evidence of some kind?

"What do you plan to do with it?" Bentley asked.

"I'm going to pick up where Winston left off and complete the filming here. This is a huge opportunity and I don't want to miss it."

I rested my chin on my knuckles and looked up at him. "But you weren't working with York on this project."

Bruce hesitated. "No. He'd unexpectedly come out of retirement for the tepen, so he didn't assemble his usual team."

"And you were no longer his usual team?" I pressed.

Bruce puffed out his impressive chest. "Not anymore. I was his successor. When he retired, he made me his heir apparent."

"Huh. Strange that no one's mentioned you."

"What do you mean?" he asked.

"I've been writing an article about York for the paper and your name hasn't come up."

"What was your relationship like with York?" Bentley asked, scooting his chair closer to me. "He always struck me as a genteel intellectual."

Bruce grunted. "Sure. That sounds good."

"You don't agree?" Bentley sounded aggrieved.

"Never meet your heroes, Bentley," I advised.

"Look, don't quote me on this because I don't like to speak ill of the dead and I owe the guy a debt of gratitude for my career…"

"But," I prompted. There was definitely a huge BUT coming and I was eager to hear it.

"But the tepen should've been *my* big break," Bruce continued. "Winston wasn't supposed to come out of retirement. Ever. When he put away his camera, he promised he was done for good."

"But he couldn't resist the lure of the tepen," I said.

"I can hardly blame him," Bentley added. "York probably waited his whole life for an opportunity like this one."

"So have I!" Bruce's eyes blazed with anger. "I finally get my big break and he tried to take it away from me. This is a once-in-a-lifetime opportunity for me too. It could totally make my career and help me establish a following. I thought it would be easy once Winston left, but it wasn't."

"It takes time," I said. "I'm sure York wasn't a household name when he first started."

Bruce balled his hands into fists. "Except I'm not just starting out. I bided my time for years, waiting to come out from behind Winston's shadow. To say I was disappointed would be an understatement. I thought it would be a seamless transition and instead I've spent the past year feeling like I was some newbie starting from scratch."

"There's still time," Bentley said. "No one's found the tepen or its nest yet."

"Exactly," Bruce said. "If I can be the one to capture the event, I can make a name for myself."

"Sounds like you're pretty desperate," I said. Desperate enough to kill his former boss to make it happen?

"This has been my whole life's focus." Bruce sighed. "I mean, everyone thinks I lack Winston's..." He flicked a gaze at Bentley. "How did you put it—genteel intellectualism? Whatever that is, I don't have it."

"Not the way you look, no," I agreed.

Bruce's eyes narrowed to slits. "What's wrong with the way I look?"

I rolled my chair backward a few inches. "I didn't say anything was wrong with it. You have a different appeal. That's all. Winston York was like the kindly old professor with a dusty tome tucked under his arm. You're like..." I flung a hand in his direction. "Adam Levine in the 70's."

Bruce and Bentley exchanged confused glances.

"My point is that your style is different from York's and so you're bound to attract different audiences," I continued.

"But we do the same job. I'm as dedicated to bringing attention to rare supernatural creatures as Winston ever was. They're the blood in my veins." He held out his arm as though I might catch a glimpse of tiny supernatural critters.

"Look, I'm not passing any judgment. You're probably the most interesting elf I've ever met."

Bentley made a disgruntled noise behind me.

"Did you know that *I* was the one who actually tracked the location of the gamora in South Africa?" Bruce asked. "That ended up being one of Winston's most famous segments and it wouldn't have happened without me. But who got the credit? Oh, that's right. Winston York." He straightened and pretended to adjust an invisible bow tie. "I'm Winston and the public adores me because they think I have some kind of magical connection to rare species when, in fact, I relied on others to do my work for me and took all the glory."

"I guess you would say you're pretty bitter," I said. Maybe bitter and desperate enough to make sure York would never come out of retirement again. Bruce would certainly have the knowledge and access required to poison York in a way that looked reminiscent of the tepen.

"I'm sad about his death, okay? It's not like I wished him any ill will. He was my mentor. What happened is a tragedy."

"Did you at least see him one last time when you arrived in town?" I asked.

"Of course. I couldn't possibly come to Starry Hollow and not see him."

I leveled a gaze at him. "But you came because you heard about the tepen sighting, right? You were probably surprised to learn that he was dusting off his camera."

Bruce hung his head. "I admit, when I stopped by his house, I was surprised and disappointed when Mabel said he was out doing prep work. She didn't seem pleased about it either."

I bit back a smile. "No, she definitely wasn't."

"I found Winston at the beach," Bruce said. "He'd discovered tepen tracks in the sand and was trying to figure out which direction it went."

"And how would you characterize your conversation with him? Was it cordial? Friendly?"

"Friendly enough."

A thought occurred to me. "You're not in any of the footage. Why wasn't he filming when you saw him?"

"He hadn't fully charged his camera," Bruce said with a laugh. "A rookie mistake, but understandable since he hadn't intended to use it."

"Did you see him alone?" I asked. "Was anyone with him?"

Bruce stroked his chin. "Not with him, but there was a family there watching him. They had two little kids who were interested in what Winston was doing. He made them keep a respectful distance so they didn't disturb the area, but they were determined little suckers."

"How so?" I asked.

"They were there when I arrived and still there when I left."

"And that's the only time you saw York?" I asked.

Bruce stared ahead, seemingly lost in thought. "Yeah, and the last time too."

"Any idea what the name of the family is?" I asked.

"Why would you need that?" His expression relaxed. "Oh, they're probably in the background of some of the footage. I'll need their permission to include them." He wagged a finger at me. "Good thinking. I'm pretty sure the wife called the husband something weird, like Colgate."

Bentley reached over and smacked my arm. "Colgate Bannon. He's got a wife and two kids."

Bruce gave us an impatient look. "Any chance you'd be willing to point me in the direction of the sheriff's office?"

"Sure." I gave him walking directions and made a mental note to text the sheriff as soon as he left. "Sheriff Nash is an agreeable guy as long as you don't aggravate him."

"Thanks for the tip." As he turned to leave, the owl turned its head another 180 degrees. Freaky.

Once he was gone, I turned to Bentley. "Now I know what kind of tattoo I want."

"*You* want a tattoo?"

I patted my bicep. "Linda Blair's face right here. Turns evil and spits out pea soup down my arm."

Bentley appeared horrified. "Is that a New Jersey thing?"

I maintained a neutral expression. "Yes, Bentley. It's the symbol on the state flag."

He inched his chair away. "Remind me never to go there."

"How well do you know Colgate and his family?"

"Shouldn't it be up to Bruce to get the releases signed?"

"Oh, sure. I was just thinking they might be good to talk to for my article since they were among the last paranormals to see York alive."

"Their house isn't far from the beach. They've got a cool swing in their yard. It goes right over the water."

"That sounds dangerous." The thought of Marley falling

off a swing and plunging into the ocean filled me with icy dread.

"Not for them. They're merfolk."

"But they live on land?"

"His wife and kids are only half."

I made a note of their address in my phone and reclaimed my hat and sunglasses.

"You can't call them?" he queried.

"I was planning to," I lied, "but now I really want to see that swing."

CHAPTER SIXTEEN

THE SWING WAS every bit as impressive as Bentley claimed. The house was partially built into the cliff and the swing was positioned to dangle over the water. The seat was large enough for four adult-sized paranormals. In fact, the entire property seemed designed for fun and games. There was a pool, a huge fire pit, and an area that resembled a volleyball court, although I'd never seen volleyball played in Starry Hollow.

An attractive man appeared on the brick patio on the side of the house. He reminded me of a surfer with his tousled hair and casual beachwear. As he opened the top of the grill, I waved to catch his attention. He looked over and smiled.

"You lost?" he called.

I jogged over. "No, sorry to interrupt. I'm Ember Rose, a reporter for the local paper. I'm writing a story about Winston York."

His expression crumpled. "Can you believe it? We were gutted when we heard the news. We'd just seen him the day before." He glanced over his shoulder toward the house. "I think my kids are still stunned."

"You're Colgate Bannon, right?"

"That's right." His brow furrowed. "Why do you want to ask us about Winston? We didn't know him."

"No, but you were among the last paranormals to see him alive. I was wondering if you could tell me about your interactions that day."

"Not much in the way of interactions. He asked us to keep a respectful distance, so we did. The kids were obsessed with watching him work though. They didn't want to leave."

"I understand you were there when his mentee came to see him—an elf named Bruce Magill. Brown shaggy hair and an owl tattoo."

Colgate nodded. "Yeah, the tattoo was awesome. I'm thinking about getting one myself. A nice octopus across my back where the tentacles wrap around me." He patted the sides of his chest.

"Dad, is the grill ready yet?" A boy with golden hair ran onto the patio. He skidded to a stop when he noticed me. "We have company."

"We do," Colgate said. "She's a reporter."

"Cool," the boy said, his eyes were like saucers.

Colgate patted the boy on the head. "Here, Shep. You take over the grill while I talk to the nice lady."

I balked. "Isn't he a little young to handle an open flame?"

Shep grinned at his dad. "You'd better not tell her you let me drive."

I laughed until I realized that the boy wasn't joking. "How old are you?"

"Age is just a number," Colgate said. "Our parenting philosophy is—if they're ready to do something, they do it."

Okay then.

"Want to watch me jump off the swing into the ocean?" Shep asked with a wisp of hopefulness.

"Not right now, thanks." I wasn't in the mood for a heart attack.

"Kid's a natural," Colgate said.

"A natural what?"

"You name it. That's why we were so excited to see Winston that day. He was a real inspiration for our boys. I can see Shep or Bryce going the explorer route. They're both fearless and inquisitive kids."

I watched with a pang of envy as Shep expertly placed meat patties on the grill. I had no doubt that little kid was a better cook than I was.

A second boy emerged from the house carrying a glass pitcher filled with blue liquid. It was so big that it blocked my view of his head and chest.

I rushed forward. "Here. Let me help."

The boy craned his neck to scoff at me. "I don't need help."

"Bryce can handle it, Ms. Rose. He's stronger than he looks."

The boy set the pitcher on the table without spilling a drop. I didn't even use glasses made of actual glass when Marley was younger. I'd been too paranoid that we'd drop one and she'd step on a shard that we missed during cleanup and she'd end up needing stitches in her foot. Hmm. I was beginning to understand where some of her anxiety had originated.

"I want cheese on mine," Bryce called to his brother.

"So, they're not in school?" I asked.

"We homeschool," Colgate said. "I know that's not the popular choice in Starry Hollow where the schools are so good, but our boys march to their own beat. My wife and I didn't want to stifle that."

"That's a huge commitment on your part," I said. I would

have been terrible at homeschooling Marley. She was much better off with actual teachers.

Colgate gave Bryce's shoulder a playful squeeze. "We love it. We have the luxury of working from home and flexible schedules, so it makes sense for us."

"You don't get overwhelmed by it all?" I asked. I got overwhelmed watching Marley do her homework in the evenings.

Shep flipped the patties and handed his father the spatula. "Race you, Bryce!" He bolted for the swing, scrambling over the edge of the brick patio and leaping onto the oversized seat. His momentum propelled him forward, out and over the water, where he proceeded to dive headfirst into the ocean below.

Colgate didn't even flinch. "Are you hungry for lunch? We have plenty of food."

I was too distracted to respond. What if Shep hit his head on a boulder? What if a shark happened to be passing by as he plunged into the water? It took me a moment to regain my composure. "You're not going to check on him?"

"He's fine," Colgate said.

"Do I have time to swing?" Bryce asked.

Colgate examined one of the patties. "One jump, but hurry back up."

"Are there steps in the cliff?" I asked. "How do they get back up?"

"They climb."

My mouth dropped open. "They...climb like little Spiderboys?"

He grinned. "Like I said, they're fearless and very agile."

I shook my head in an effort to refocus. "Did you notice Winston accept anything from the man you saw? A drink? A vial? Anything at all?"

"No, but you can check Bryce's recording. He never

stopped filming the poor guy. I wasn't about to tell him to stop though." He gave me a sheepish grin. "Don't want to be responsible for quashing their talents. The world will do enough of that."

Colgate's wife stepped onto the patio with a stack of empty plates. "Oh, hello. I didn't realize we had company."

I gave her an awkward wave. "Sorry to intrude."

"Marsali, this is Ember," he said and frowned. "Apologies but I've forgotten your last name already."

"Rose," I said.

Marsali's lashes fluttered in surprise. "Rose? Not *the* Rose."

"Afraid so. Hyacinth is my aunt."

She set the plates on the table, her eyes still trained on me. "That makes you a descendant of the One True Witch."

I shrugged nonchalantly. "So I've been told."

"Marsali, would you mind grabbing Bryce's recording? Ms. Rose would like to look at it for an article she's writing."

"Sure thing. I'll be right back."

"Your place is really nice," I said.

"Yeah, it's a great location. Convenient to town but still private. The beach is only a short walk."

Marsali returned with the camera and handed it to me. "It's all teed up."

I hit play and watched the footage of Bruce and York. Like the tepen, they never touched or exchanged items of any kind. There was nothing that indicated Bruce had poisoned his former mentor.

"Thank you. That's helpful." I returned the camera as the boys emerged from the side of the cliff soaking wet and wearing matching smiles. It occurred to me that Aspen and Ackley might benefit from some playtime with the Bannon boys. I'd have to mention it to Aster.

"Do you want to try?" Shep asked.

I laughed. "I don't think so. My will hasn't been updated... or written."

"Go on, Ember," Marsali urged gently. "You're a Rose. You can do anything."

I blinked at her. It felt odd that this woman—this stranger —believed in me. Not because she had expectations or an air of superiority that needed to be supported but simply because she looked at me and didn't find me wanting. It was such a foreign concept that I had a hard time accepting it.

"Jump! Jump!" The boys chanted and clapped their hands in sync.

"I do love flying on my broomstick," I said, which was true. That was about as far as the daredevil inside me was willing to go.

"You must have such incredible magic," Marsali said. "I bet you could slide down on a rainbow if you wanted to."

I laughed at the image of me gliding down the arch of a rainbow into the sea. "I don't know about that. I've made it rain, but no rainbows."

"Just one time, please?" Shep asked, folding his hands together in mock prayer.

Darn, those boys were too cute for their own good.

"Get on the swing, and if it's too intimidating, then stay on and don't jump," Colgate suggested.

"I've never rappelled," I said. "How will I get back up?"

"I bet you know a levitation spell or something," Bryce said. "I can record you too. That way you can show your friends."

I could show Marley. It would be a great example of taking a leap of faith. "Fine, you've convinced me. I'll do it."

The boys cheered and Colgate pulled the lid over the grill. "These'll keep a few minutes more."

I strolled across the yard to the swing, ignoring the intense beating of my heart. A leap into the unknown. I'd done it before when I'd accepted my cousins' hand to escape to Starry Hollow. I could do this.

I kicked off my shoes and settled on the swing, getting comfortable. I began to rock back and forth, building momentum. As I pitched forward, I looked down at the water below and stifled a gasp. What was I thinking?

"Jump!" the boys shouted.

I swung out over the water and let go.

The fall was both terrifying and exhilarating. I hit the water feet first and plunged a few feet before returning to the surface. I glanced up to see four heads peering over the side. I gave an exaggerated wave and they cheered.

Bobbing in the water, I felt more alive than I had in ages. I hadn't even realized I'd been sticking to the confines of my comfort zone until now. Not straying from my daily routine, no matter how crazy it made me. Resisting the urge to use the full extent of my powers as well as Ivy's. I realized now that I'd been afraid. Afraid of what would happen if I opened those floodgates. Afraid of my aunt's wrath and of acceptance. Afraid of change.

I gazed at the seemingly insurmountable cliffside.

"One that would have the fruit must first climb the tree...or cliff," I said, echoing Raoul's fortune cookie coaching.

As I began the slippery climb back up to the Bannon house, I knew that I wasn't afraid anymore. Whatever awaited me when I opened a new door, I could handle it.

I focused on my magic and drew it to me. "*Levo*," I said with an air of confidence. Energy boosted me higher so that I was halfway up the cliffside when I spotted a trail of seaweed spilling out of a deep crevice. I poked my head as far as it would go and peered inside. A gasp escaped me.

"You clever girl."

It was a nest unlike any other, where no nest should be. It

179

was made of seaweed and barnacles and nestled safely inside was a single egg.

There was no sign of the tepen. I surveyed the area, searching for evidence that the adult tepen had passed this way. There was no obvious route, only the seaweed and the nest itself. No wonder no one had discovered it yet. Poor Deputy Bolan. The leprechaun never stood a chance.

"Good to see you, little fella," I whispered and continued my way up to the top. I didn't tell the Bannons what I found. Instead, I used a drying spell on my clothes and gave Bryce my number so he could send me the video. I couldn't wait to share it with Marley, but first, there was something far more important I had to do.

An hour later, I returned to the cliffside with Jarek Heidelberg and Bruce Magill. I'd made a deal with both of them that I would show them the location of the nest if they promised to leave town afterward so that the others would follow. The business owners took their cue from trackers like Bruce. If they thought there was no point in remaining in Starry Hollow, they'd pack up and go.

Bruce and I sat on my broomstick and I lowered us to the crevice. An expert climber, Jarek opted to scale down the cliffside.

"You can't reveal you have footage until everyone has left town," I reminded Bruce as he recorded our descent.

"I can't thank you enough," he said. "This one piece might inspire a whole new generation of explorers."

"Not too bad for your career either," I said.

The tree nymph shushed us as he peered inside the fissure.

"The egg looks good. The first crack is visible, which means it's healthy enough to hatch soon." He shifted aside so that I could steer Bruce closer to capture the moment—but not the egg.

"As long as no one else finds this place, there will be a new tepen in the world soon," Jarek said.

"Except that means we lose the adult tepen," I said. It hardly seemed fair—this one in and one out policy. No wonder they were so rare. They needed to lay multiple eggs if they were going to survive as a species.

Jarek looked at me. "You sound sad about that."

"Of course. It's sad, right?"

"Yes," he agreed. "It is."

"Will the baby tepen stay here?" I asked.

"No, once it hatches and the adult tepen leaves, the baby will return to the ocean to feed and grow," Bruce said.

I watched as Bruce reviewed the recording on his screen. "There's so much in this world that's still a mystery," I said.

"That's what keeps it interesting," Bruce said. "If we know everything, we stop learning. If we stop learning, we cease to grow."

I shifted the broomstick so that I could get one last glimpse of the fragile egg. "Welcome to the world, little buddy. Enjoy the ride."

CHAPTER SEVENTEEN

I WAS SO ELATED by my personal and professional break-throughs that I rode that high straight to York's house to deliver the exciting news to his wife. I thought it might offer her some kind of closure to know that Bruce Magill would finally be taking the torch lit by his mentor.

Mabel opened the door and a cat shot past my feet.

"Oh, crap." In my defense, that cat was much faster than PP3.

"Don't worry. He won't go far. They're just excited now that they can roam freely." She ushered me inside. "What brings you back?"

"I'm sorry to interrupt. I thought you'd be happy to know that we found the tepen's nest. I also wanted to fact check a few notes I gathered on your husband before I finish my article. Would you mind?"

"I'd love to help. Why don't you come in and have a cup of tea?"

"Oh, sure. If you don't mind the company."

"It would be nice, to be honest. Winston was such a

hermit that we didn't often receive visitors. Now that he's gone, it's a bit lonely."

"I can imagine." When Karl died, I'd had to focus on Marley. There'd been no time to feel lonely.

I trailed after her to the kitchen and lingered at the other end of the counter while Mabel put the kettle on. A book peeked out from beneath a pile of unopened mail. I could just make out the first part of the title—*Rare and*.

I slid the book out from beneath the mail. Sure enough, it was the copy of *Rare and Dangerous* that Delphine had dropped off.

"Oh, hey. The librarian mentioned that she'd dropped this off. If you want, I can return it for you. Save you a trip."

The kettle came to a boil and she switched off the burner. "I didn't know it was there. Winston always had his books scattered everywhere. They became part of the furniture."

I paged through the book while Mabel made the tea. It was a comprehensive book with print so small I needed reading glasses. My stomach turned at the thought of needing reading glasses.

"I'm too young," I murmured and kept skimming. I paused when I noticed a crease in a top corner of a page and frowned. A dog-eared page? Winston was going straight to Hell, apparently. As I went to turn the page, my gaze fell on a familiar phrase and I froze.

Vasuki.

Another memory shifted into place.

"Hey, Mabel. Would you mind if I had another look in the workshop? I just remembered something that would be helpful for my article."

She gave me a curious look. "I suppose that would be fine. I can bring the tea to you there if you like. My husband always took his tea in there. I can't remember the last time we sat in here together."

"That would be great, thanks." I hurried to the workshop, my head spinning. I'd been so overwhelmed the first time I was here that I hadn't fully registered all the information in front of me.

The workshop appeared untouched since my last visit. I crossed the workshop to the wall where the jars still sat. Nestled between jars labeled *siduri* and *patecatl* was one labeled *vasuki*.

So York had made contact with a vasuki demon serpent and had the poison to prove it. But why would he have earmarked the page in *Rare and Dangerous*? Had he accidentally poisoned himself and was looking for a cure? No, that didn't make sense.

"Here you are, dear. I'll set this down for you and you drink it when you're ready."

I turned to see Mabel carrying a mug to one of the tables. "Thank you. I have a quick question, if you don't mind. Did your husband seem well to you in the days before he died?"

She placed the mug on a coaster and faced me. "How do you mean?"

I tried to recall the symptoms I'd seen mentioned in connection with vasuki poison. "Did he complain of any nausea or dizziness?"

She appeared thoughtful. "Now that you mention it, he complained of a headache the morning before he left." She stopped talking, her eyes moist. "In fact, I suggested he stay home until he was better, but that's not how Winston operated, so I simply gave him the letter to mail and he was on his way."

I turned back to contemplate the jars.

"You should drink your tea before it gets cold." She laughed softly. "I was forever saying that to Winston."

Not wanting to be impolite, I went to the table to retrieve the drink. As I reached over the mug to turn the handle toward me, my bracelet plunged into the tea, splashing the liquid onto the table.

Crap on a cracker. I couldn't tell Raoul or I'd never hear the end of it. "I'm so sorry." I pulled a tissue from my pocket and dabbed at the wet spots on the table.

"It's fine, dear. I'll clean it up."

I fished the bracelet out of the brown liquid and placed it on the tissue to dry. As I went to lift the mug, I noticed that the bright green emerald had faded to celadon. Icy tendrils of dread spread throughout my body.

Poison.

There was poison in my tea.

I tried to disguise my shock as the realization settled in.

Mabel York killed her husband.

She watched me closely, so I lifted the mug to my lips and pretended to drink.

"Nice and warm, just the way I like it," I said. "Any special herbs? It has a slightly bitter taste."

"I suppose vasuki might taste bitter. I've never tried it myself."

I feigned ignorance. "I've never heard of vasuki."

"No? Isn't that what you came in here to look for?" She inclined her head toward the jar. "It's right over there on the shelf. Was a bugger to open that lid, so I used a little magic and it popped right off."

"You know what's in the jar?" I queried. "I thought you weren't allowed in here."

"I'm not completely ignorant. I was married for far too long not to pick up information here and there."

"Here and there, like here in the workshop and a book from the library?"

"You can drop the act. I knew as soon as you showed up on my doorstep that you'd figured it out."

I played along. "I guess we're two clever ladies then."

185

Her lips curled into a cruel smile. "Winston didn't have a clue. He was far too preoccupied with his comeback." Her brow creased. "I expected you to be dead by now. I think you should drink more."

I shrugged. "I disappoint a lot of folks. Get in line." I picked up my bracelet and slipped it into my bag. "So what happened? You were so resentful that he went back to work that you killed him?"

"I suppose I might as well tell you. You won't be walking out of here alive anyway."

"If it's any consolation, I'm dizzy," I lied. "I feel a headache coming on." I leaned against the table for good measure. I figured if she thought I was dying, then she'd lower her defenses.

"That's how I felt when Winston announced that he wanted a divorce."

My eyes popped. "Whoa. What?"

"That's right. After forty-five years of marriage. Of me waiting patiently while he lives his life and pursues *his* dreams that don't appear to include me. *Now* he has the gall to want to file for divorce?" Mabel's eyes gleamed with righteous anger.

"I can understand why that upset you." A heat-of-the-moment whack on the head with a skillet I could almost understand, but Mabel actually planned his murder.

"I asked him if there was another woman. I didn't see how that was possible since he never left the house, but still. Maybe he was spending time in chat rooms. Who knows what he was doing in the workshop?"

"And was there—another woman?"

Her voice trembled as she spoke. "No. He said he wanted to live the rest of his life alone. That we'd run our course and it was time to move on from the marriage."

Wow. I wasn't sure which one was worse—to be left for

someone else in the twilight of my life or to be left for no one at all.

"That had to hurt."

"It was unbearable," she seethed. "There was no way I was letting him waltz out of our marriage. I'd invested most of my life in that man and what did I have to show for it? Bottles of poisons and a useless collection of horns?"

"And so you killed Winston with one of his own poisons."

She barked a short laugh. "Ironic, isn't it?"

"More like opportunistic. How did you do it? A shot in his morning coffee? Mixed in with the honey in his porridge? The green smoothie?"

"I'd put it in his tea that morning, like I did with yours, but he was so excited about the tepen that he refused food and drink. I panicked."

I thought of the stack of mail on top of the *Rare and Dangerous* book. "The stamp. You said that you asked him to mail an envelope on his way out that morning and that he had to put on the stamp. You laced the back with the poison, knowing he'd lick it just before he left the house. He'd send off the evidence and manage to die elsewhere, far away from you." I couldn't resist giving her a look of admiration. "Nice work."

"He thought he was the clever one, always drumming up creative ways of tracking and trapping his prey. Did he really think I'd go along with his plans without a fight?"

"Except it wasn't a fight. You killed him."

"I simply helped him with population control."

"Wow. That's cold, Mabel."

"Not as cold as the way he treated me." Her angry expression melted into one of pain. "He didn't deserve me."

"No, he didn't. But he also didn't deserve to die because of it."

She wiped away a stray tear and took a menacing step forward. "Why aren't you dead yet?"

"It took an hour or so for Winston to die, didn't it?" I sat on the stool at the table. "I guess we should make ourselves comfortable."

"I'd be happy to hasten things along. Fairies have magic too, you know. Even halflings like me." She pulled a sparkling wand from behind her and aimed it at me.

"You do realize a wand like that lacks the intimidation factor. It looks like you're going to glitter me to death."

"I don't need to intimidate you. I only need to kill you."

"Just so you know, even if you weren't going to the Bad Place for killing Winston, you'd still be going there for dog-earing a library book."

"How did you figure out it wasn't the tepen? That's what everyone else believes."

"Only because they didn't watch the video," I said. "The sheriff and I saw that the tepen never made contact with him and I found him straight afterward."

She blanched. "The sheriff knows it was murder?"

I nodded. "He and I have been investigating together."

Her fingers tightened around the wand. "Then the poison won't work. I need to do something else or he'll figure it out."

Oops, that was probably the wrong thing to reveal. I thought I could buy a little more time, but this was my cue to leave. I reached for my bag.

"Not so fast!" Magic streaked from her wand and I ducked. The blue light zapped a picture on the wall and cracked the glass.

I ran.

The sound of glass shattering seemed to punctuate each step. Jars and bottles exploded. I crawled across the floor to hide beneath a table. Glass crashed on the floor around me and shards skidded toward my hands. I yanked my hands away to avoid getting cut.

The only exit was being blocked by Mabel. That meant my only option was to move her out of the way. I tried to remember the strength spell I'd done with Wren. To be fair, I could probably overpower Mabel anyway, but I needed to get close to her and her zap-happy wand prevented that.

"I'm going to torch this workshop to the ground and you along with it," Mabel said, her voice shaking with fury. "There will be no evidence. No proof. Just another tragic accident. I'll make it look as though I wasn't even here when it happened. Everyone knows you're writing an article. They'll think you were in here snooping."

I had flashbacks to the night I arrived in Starry Hollow—the fire in my New Jersey apartment. If it hadn't been for my cousins, we would have died. Looking around right now, I knew that no one was coming to save me. I had to get out of this on my own.

I *would* get out of this on my own.

Across the room, Winston's trophies seemed to call to me. I viewed them differently now. He hadn't killed these creatures and had them stuffed and mounted. They'd died and he'd preserved their memories. He'd worshipped them. Devoted his life to them.

For a fleeting moment, I considered trying to body swap with one of the larger creatures, but I worried about leaving my physical form unattended. Another idea formed, but I wasn't sure if it was even possible.

You're a Rose. You can do anything.

I wasn't so sure Marsali was right about *anything*, but I knew I had more magic in me than I'd felt comfortable using.

Until now.

I concentrated on the life-sized creatures and let the magic flow freely. Let it build within me until I was ready to release it. I hoped I'd chosen the right word or this could easily backfire. Hell, even if it *was* the right word, it could still backfire.

I pushed my hands toward the far wall. "*Excito!*"

Each and every rare supernatural creature seemed to groan at once. They peeled themselves off the wall, their eyes fixed on Mabel. She backed away, her mouth agape. She raised a shaky hand and aimed her wand at them.

"Stop right there," she yelled.

But they wouldn't answer to her. They were my zombie horde.

I tried to move from under the table, but she quickly shifted the wand back to me. "You're not going anywhere."

One of the bear-sized creatures lunged at her, its claws as sharp now as they were when it was alive. She screamed and dropped her wand.

I took a chance and rushed forward. I scooped up her wand and pointed it at her. She was on the floor now, struggling beneath the weight of the creature.

"*Desisto*," I said firmly.

The creature froze and I nudged it aside, the wand still aimed at Mabel.

"Why don't you just leave me alone?" she sobbed. "You're going to die anyway."

"Oh, did I forget to tell you? I didn't drink your tea, Mabel. I'll live to annoy another day. You might as well sit tight while I call the sheriff. One move and I'll have these creatures back in action."

She lowered the back of her head to the floor in defeat. "How did you do that?" she whispered. "In all my years, I've never seen anything like it."

I pulled out my phone and dialed the sheriff. "My name is Ember Rose," I said proudly, "and I'm a descendant of the One True Witch."

CHAPTER EIGHTEEN

"The weather is so lovely today, I thought we could spend time on the veranda."

"Sounds good to me." I followed my aunt outside with a drink in my hand. She'd invited me to Thornhold for a chat and I waited anxiously to see what was on her mind. With Aunt Hyacinth, you could never be too sure.

"How is Marley's herb garden coming along? I keep thinking I should drop by to see her progress, but I don't wish to intrude."

"Oh, you know you can drop by any time." Sort of. Maybe call first—with twenty-four hours' notice. "She's doing a great job with the garden. Even Calla was impressed. It seems to be her thing."

My aunt regarded me. "But not yours?"

I swatted a hand in the air. "No, definitely not mine. I still manage to kill artificial flowers, so it's best to keep the natural world safe from my impact."

Tell her the appetizers are delicious.

Raoul? What are you doing here?

Accountability coach, remember? I followed you. Tell her they taste like stale pizza crust from the top of the heap.

I cringed. *You realize that's not a compliment, right?*

It is in my world.

Inwardly, I sighed. I knew Raoul meant well, but it was time to reclaim my headspace. I was feeling more centered, stronger than ever, in fact, and I knew I could handle this without his input.

Raoul, you know I love you…

Let me guess. You don't want me to be your accountability coach anymore.

Would you be disappointed? It isn't that I don't appreciate your contributions, but there are some things I need to handle on my own and I can't think straight when you're constantly popping into my head with advice. I don't want to lose myself.

No, it's cool. To be honest, I don't think I'm cut out for it. I was starting to resent having to give you so much attention when really I just want to focus on me.

I laughed. *So we're good?*

I'm your familiar. You can't get rid of me that easily.

My aunt tilted her head. "Is something funny, Ember?"

"Oh, no. Well, yes, but nothing I can repeat. It was a bawdy joke I heard recently." I figured I was safe. No way would Aunt Hyacinth dare ask me to repeat a bawdy joke.

"I see."

Raoul? I peered at the hedge, but there was no sign of the raccoon. Phew. At least we navigated that without too much fallout. It was only when I returned my attention to my aunt that I realized she was staring at me with a strange expression.

"Do I have crumbs stuck on my lip?" I made a half-hearted attempt to brush away any offensive bits.

"What? No. I was simply thinking about something I heard."

"You heard a bawdy joke too? What are the odds?"

She ignored my remark. "You mentioned your impact on the natural world and that reminded me." The intensity of Aunt Hyacinth's gaze made me feel like a bug under a microscope—or maybe like a hostess at the restaurant that tried to seat her too close to the kitchen.

"Oh?"

My aunt sipped her cocktail, her keen eyes still assessing me. "I've noticed a difference in you lately myself."

I tried to keep my game face on. "Really? I have been using a new deodorant. It's missing that fresh powder scent."

"Don't test my patience, Ember. If you're finally fully embracing your powers, I'm thrilled. It means my efforts haven't been in vain."

I relaxed slightly.

"All your tutors have mentioned your impressive strides recently, in fact." She lifted her glass to her lips and peered at me over the rim. "It made me curious."

Uh oh.

"I've gotten more comfortable in my own skin," I said, which was true.

"And how is your familiar? There've been no more issues with the other animal, the bossy one?"

"Gilbert? No, that's all done and dusted." I knew this wasn't a polite inquiry. My aunt was reminding me of the incident with the mobster animal and her role in resolving it because it was time to collect.

We stood in mutual silence for a moment, staring at each other.

My aunt spoke first. "I think it's time you told me the truth, don't you? It's not as though you can hide it forever."

I drained the glass and set it on the stone wall at my hip. It was time to come clean.

"I have Ivy's Book of Shadows."

193

It was the first time I'd ever seen my aunt look gobs-macked. "Is that so?" she asked, quickly recovering her poise.

"That's so. I also have access to her magic." I paused. "All of it."

She regarded me coolly. "I don't know how you managed that, but it's no matter. I'd like you to go back to the cottage and bring me the items. The wand, the grimoire, *and* the Book of Shadows."

"Why? You gave two of those to Marley and I found the other one. They don't belong to you."

Her withering gaze struck fear in my heart, but I steeled myself against it. "Yarrow…"

"Ember."

Her nostrils flared. "Ember, I am the head of this family and I demand that you return the items to me at once. They are family heirlooms."

"That you gave away to other members of the family."

"And now I want them back."

"I knew it! The whole reason you gave them to Marley was because you thought she would be able to unlock them and access the magic. Well, surprise, Auntie. It was me, not Marley. I did it." I jabbed my thumb into my chest.

"Ivy's power is of no use to you," she said. "I'm a much more worthy recipient."

"If you're a better recipient, then why weren't you able to access the magic yourself? Why did you have to wait for years until someone came along who could do the job? Your own children couldn't even do it."

Aunt Hyacinth didn't seem to like this response. "Have I not given you and your daughter a comfortable home? A job? Respectability?"

Like I cared about respectability. "I thought that was because we're family, not because you wanted something from us." Although she was shorter than me, right now she seemed about ten feet tall.

"Ember, I am asking you nicely."

"And I am telling you no. Nicely. Thank you for the drink. I'll show myself out." I turned on my heel and marched toward the house.

"Mark my words Ember," she called after me. "I will acquire Ivy's magic, with or without your permission."

I barked a short laugh and turned to look at her. "I'd like to see you try." With those parting words, I left Thornhold.

"I can't believe you did that." Marley stared at the screen where the video of my impressive leap of faith had just finished. I decided to tell her about my unpleasant conversation with Aunt Hyacinth another time. For now, I just wanted to enjoy this time with my daughter.

"I'm fearless, didn't you know?"

She beamed as though she'd done the jump herself. "Can I watch it again?"

I laughed. "Later. It's getting late and you need to finish your homework."

PP3 began to bark wildly.

"I guess we have a visitor," I said, pushing back my chair. "I'll see who it is."

I opened the door to reveal my familiar. "Raoul? Why are you knocking?"

He seemed animated, pointing excitedly to some distant location.

"What is it, boy? Did Florian get drunk and fall down a well?" I asked.

Marley joined me at the door. "He wants us to go somewhere."

"Clearly. His thoughts are so jumbled that I can't understand him."

Raoul scurried over to the car and pawed at the door. One word flashed clearly in my mind.

Tepen.

"Hurry, Marley." I grabbed my keys and fled the cottage.

Balefire Beach, he said, starting to calm down as he climbed into the backseat.

"Did you run all the way here?" I asked.

He nodded in the rearview mirror. Marley buckled up and we sped toward the beach just in time to catch the sunset. I smiled as we chased after Raoul amidst the burning hues of red, pink, orange, and yellow that streaked across the sky.

"Mom, there!"

A lone creature slithered across the sand. With its hawk head, long serpentine body, and rattle tail, it was like nothing I'd ever seen. I slowed to a stop, wanting to keep a respectful distance.

"If this is the last view the tepen has, I think it chose well," I said. I clasped Marley's hand on my right and Raoul's paw on my left. Together, we watched as the creature crawled across the sand. As the sun dipped below the horizon, the tepen reached the water.

Marley sniffed. "Isn't there anything we can do?"

"This is life," I said quietly. "It's a hard lesson, but we have to let go of the things we can't control." The tepen knew that. Its whole job was to live long enough to help the next generation come into existence and then go softly into that good night. If that's not letting go, I don't know what is.

"Sounds like a lesson Aunt Hyacinth still needs to learn."

"You don't know the half of it." That was a story for another day.

"Maybe that's why she's such a bitter and unhappy witch,"

Marley said. "She refuses to let go and it's making her miserable."

Her words pierced my heart. Under no circumstances did I want to become like Aunt Hyacinth. She managed to push everyone away by trying to control the relationships, by setting conditions instead of accepting her loved ones as they are. As happy as she seemed with Craig at the moment, I suspected that relationship, too, would eventually suffer, once the honeymoon period ended. Although I wasn't quite to my aunt's level, I realized that I, too, tried to control certain relationships to produce my desired outcome and it wasn't healthy.

I don't want to end up miserable and alone.

The tepen splashed its way through the surf until its head disappeared. Our last glimpse of the magnificent creature was of its tail as a wave crashed over it, swallowing it completely.

Darkness now blanketed the beach, but I remained rooted to the sand. It was a strange moment, knowing I'd just witnessed the end of a life. I felt more admiration for the tepen than I ever thought possible. It did what needed to be done no matter how difficult the task.

Marley leaned against me the same way she had a thousand times before. "I love you, Mom."

I stroked her hair. "I love you, too."

What about me? Raoul asked. *I found the tepen.*

I smiled at the raccoon. "And I'd love you even if you hadn't. It's called unconditional love." Aunt Hyacinth should try it sometime.

Raoul fixed his dark eyes on me. *I'd love you even if you didn't feed me...but I'm glad that you do.*

The three of us continued to hold hands as we slowly made our way back across the beach, making the most of our time together. I looked skyward at the twinkling lights above, inhaled deeply, and thanked my lucky stars.

* * *

Don't miss *Magic & Misfits*, Book 13 in the series.

You can also like me on Facebook so you can find out about the next book before it's even available.

Printed in Great Britain
by Amazon